Walking
on Ice

Alba Branca was born and raised in Paris. At seventeen, she left for America and for several years moved between France and New York, first to complete her education and later to work for several galleries. At this time she published her first articles on contemporary art, as well as her first short story.

Alba Branca, her husband and son now live in London where she is currently working on her second novel.

ALSO BY ALBA BRANCA

Muse

Alba Branca

Walking on Ice

PAN BOOKS

'The Yellow Slippers' was previously published in the USA
in the 1995 spring issue of *Open City* magazine

First published 2000 by Pan
an imprint of Macmillan Publishers Ltd
25 Eccleston Place, London SW1W 9NF
Basingstoke and Oxford
Associated companies throughout the world
www.macmillan.co.uk

ISBN 0 330 35267 9

1 3 5 7 9 8 6 4 2

A CIP catalogue record for this book is available from
the British Library.

Typeset by SetSystems Ltd, Saffron Walden, Essex
Printed and bound in Great Britain by
Mackays of Chatham plc, Chatham, Kent

For my mother and father

Contents

Offhand

Elsie watches the faces float around her like large butterflies, wings flapping as they smile.

Would you like a sandwich, Elsie, dear? Oh, look at how beautiful you are with that dress on. Did that gorgeous mother of yours buy you that dress?

But Bubbles Mayham leaves before Elsie can even start telling her about the blue and white frilled dress, about the exhausting day they spent in the shop where everyone was so attentive to Mother, so much so that she bought more than she could carry, and when they got home Father pulled Mother aside and slammed the bedroom door shut so that Elsie couldn't hear what they were arguing about, although she had a fair idea that it was about the shopping spree. Most of their fights were about that.

Leora, you've got a shopping problem! she heard Father shout through the wooden door.

I do not! Mother answered tearfully.

Then their voices went down again, and up, and down, and up, and down, like the squeaky see-saw in Central Park she goes to with Sylvia the nanny, who has Sundays off because she wants to be with her family.

Sylvia is Jamaican. She wears her black hair up in a bun and she irons her white frock every morning before taking care of Elsie. When she smiles her gums show and they're red like strawberries. She smiles a lot with Elsie, but not so much with Father and Mother whom she calls Mr Posner and Mrs Posner.

Sylvia brought Elsie to this party, and she's sitting over there with the other nannies. There, by the *boofett*. Elsie isn't quite sure what this means, but she knows it's something Francesca's mother, Bubbles Mayham, says whenever she approaches the long table covered with delicacies which are too high for some of the younger children to reach.

Come to the *boofett*, Caroline, darling, Bubbles says to an elegant looking woman who wears too much perfume, come here, have some more champagne, how have you been, it's been *soo* long since I've seen you . . .

The trail in the voice drags out the days they've been apart, and the shape of Bubbles' mouth when she talks is round like the spider bite Elsie got in the country when she was playing with Mackie, the next door neighbour, and she had to be rushed to the emergency room of the hospital with the pale green walls because the bite developed into an infection and Father said that could be dangerous.

Elsie loves that word, dangerous, because it arouses concern and makes her parents pay attention to her.

Bubbles Mayham, an old friend of Elsie's mother, is very rich. Her apartment looks like a palace, and in its majestic rooms there are men who roam around and who look like waiters in restaurants (Francesca calls them servants) and who wear white gloves and serve little sandwiches and drinks on high silver trays.

Bubbles is also very big and moves slowly. She looks like a beetle and when she laughs she sounds as though she has the hiccups. Elsie likes her. She's warm and friendly (much more so than her mother and father), and whenever she gives a party there's always lots of food.

Today is her daughter Francesca's seventh birthday. Francesca is Elsie's classmate and they were born a month and two days and six and a half hours apart. This makes Elsie six years, eleven months minus two days old.

Francesca is overweight and not very pretty, so the children like to make fun of her and make her cry. They like to pull her thick plaits and pretend she's a pony, and once the teacher had to detach Francesca from a tree trunk where four of the boys had tied her by wrapping a skipping rope around her, claiming she was a birthday present for the Sioux Indians to eat.

These boys were severely punished.

But when her mother throws her parties, Francesca is the queen. No one dares make fun of her, and all the children are very polite and say yes please and no thank you because they want to be invited again. Then, for the next two days or so, they're very nice to Francesca, because in their minds they still have a picture of the gilded mirrors, and the marble sinks with golden taps where the water sprinkles out like waterfalls, and the men in the white gloves, and the delicious sandwiches with little cucumbers on top, and the dark chocolate fudge cake, and the long carpeted hallways where one can run and lose oneself and end up in a totally different room.

But after those two days, things return to normal, and soon they forget and cannot tell the white gloves from the ceilings or Francesca's bedroom from her bathroom, and they start teasing her again.

Today she is queen though, and Elsie feels relieved. She doesn't like it when the children are mean to her because she likes Francesca. But she cannot tell the children her real thoughts for fear that they will start being mean to her, too. So she keeps these thoughts to herself.

Elsie is here alone with Sylvia. It has been a long time since she's attended a party without at least one of her parents, and while she was initially apprehensive about it, now she's happy she's without them. At least she doesn't have to leave early because Mother has an appointment, nor does she have to endure Mother's endless chit-chat with all the other grown-ups who all seem to know her. Actually, wherever they go, people seem to know Mother. She used to be a film star a long time ago. Now, she designs clothes.

Although Mother likes Bubbles and wanted to attend today's party, she couldn't make it because she had an important doctor's appointment. (You have to make an appointment way in advance because he's always booked up Mother says – Elsie imagines rows of books that smell of dust, which run from one end of the doctor's apartment to the other.)

Father couldn't make it because he had too many patients today. (Tuesday is always a busy day. Father is a therapist and he has explained to Elsie that people come to him and tell him about their problems which he tries to help them solve.)

So Sylvia brought her in a taxi, and now she seems to be enjoying herself with the other nannies who are discreetly nibbling on their chocolate cake.

Elsie sits on a chair and drinks her orange juice. For

some reason, maybe because she's here on her own, she feels older today. As she turns her head, she suddenly catches a glimpse of herself in the mirror on her right-hand side. She feels like saying hello to her own image but of course that's a ridiculous idea. So instead she looks around to be sure that no one has noticed her, then she turns her head back to the mirror and looks at herself intently. She decides that she likes her new dress, and the way her blonde curly hair looks in a ponytail. Actually, she feels like smiling for no apparent reason, but of course she'll hold it in like when she needs to go to the bathroom.

Mother says Elsie is vain.

Elsie likes that idea. Of being vain.

She watches the people around her. The party seems to have an equal amount of grown-ups and children. Hardly any of them seem to stand still. They all seem to be going somewhere: her classmates walk around with their coloured paper plates stacked with all kinds of food, some babies are crawling around the floor under their nannies' or their mothers' watchful eyes, and the grown-ups are moving from one person to another as if they were bored staying with the same person for too long.

One of the grown-ups, a very tall woman with short dark hair and a long blue dress, reminds Elsie of a portrait she saw at the Metropolitan Museum the other day with Mother and her cousin Ophelia who was visiting from London. Mother said that the portrait in question was painted more than a hundred years ago. This bothered Elsie. Why did the woman look so young if she was meant to be so old? she asked. Mother explained that the painting had been completed when the woman was still young and beautiful, and thus she had been immortalized. And that was what art was about, among other things. What other things? Elsie had asked, and Mother had promised to explain once they got home.

But Mother never did explain and Elsie forgot to ask.

As Elsie is watching the grown-ups at the party, she decides that they're like those paintings in the Metropolitan Museum: they speak to her, but in a way that she cannot always understand. Father doesn't seem to understand them well either, so most of the time, unless she's with Mother who's usually the one who brings Elsie to the museum, she finds herself looking at the paintings for a longer time than Father does.

One day Elsie asked Father why he took her to museums if he didn't like them.

Who says I don't like them? Father asked.

Do you like them less than Mother does?

Who says I don't like them? Father asked again.

That day Father was dressed in his corduroy pants and his soft V-necked sweater. When they left the museum he lit his pipe pensively, and as they crossed 5th Avenue he almost got both of them hit by a taxi. Elsie trembled but Father remained quiet and she couldn't understand why. She didn't bother asking, though, because she knew that he wouldn't answer her. Father didn't like to answer what he called personal questions. This one, she felt, was a personal question.

When they got home Father went into his study to make some phone calls, and when Mother got back that evening he was in a very grumpy mood and they all ate dinner in an icy silence. This was not unusual since for a few months now, Father and Mother often seemed to be grumpy with each other, and it dug a hole in Elsie's stomach, like the construction worker who was drilling the pavement on her street.

The grown-ups at the party are anything but icy. They laugh and smoke and joke, and even their seriousness is lively. As she looks at them, Elsie wishes Father was the same. Sometimes his aloofness makes her sad. She wishes he would hug her more often and tell her stories like he used to. The most affection he gives her these days is a pat on the head, or a quick kiss on the cheek where his lips feel hard and cold. As for Mother, although her smell and her smile and her voice are very present in Elsie's life, she seems to be preoccupied with something. The other day when they went shopping together, Mother took her mobile phone out of her bag three times because she said she had to make an urgent phone call (no, it's not the doctor, darling), and every time she hung up with a frown on her face because the person wasn't there.

As she is thinking these thoughts, Elsie notices a man who looks very much like Father. Except that this man seems more jovial and his hair isn't grey but brown. When he sees Elsie, his eyes seem to shine as if he recognizes her, which she finds rather peculiar.

She is interrupted by Roger, Matthew and Sophie, who come towards her. They are all in her class, and Sophie likes Roger but it's a secret. Matthew gives Elsie the rest of his cake, and as she eats it (her third helping) her stomach starts to hurt a little, but never mind.

Her classmates ask Elsie why she's sitting there all alone, and Elsie answers, I'm observing.

Roger asks her what that means and Elsie answers whatever. The children look at her inquisitively and leave her to her adult thoughts.

Decidedly Elsie thinks, I'm not a child any more. These people are nincompoops. That's what Grandma says. Elsie loves her grandmother. She visits her every Thursday after school, and on Sundays Grandma takes her to Rumpelmayer where they eat cake and ice-cream. Afterwards, they take a leisurely stroll through the park and at five o'clock exactly, Grandma brings Elsie to Mr Stratenbaum's house.

Mr Stratenbaum is Grandma's friend. He lives in a dark apartment on Central Park West and has been her friend for eleven years, ever since Grandpa died, and she's never called him by his first name. At least not in front of any of them, although Mother claims that they're more intimate in private, a concept Elsie has trouble understanding, since for her public and private are basically the same thing, like the shallow and the deep end of a swimming pool.

Mr Stratenbaum's apartment smells of old people, and he himself has trouble walking, and when he pats Elsie's cheek and says hello, my little Elsie, his hand trembles uncontrollably.

Elsie doesn't like Mr Stratenbaum. So when Grandma goes to visit him, that is when Sylvia usually picks Elsie up and brings her home.

The thought of Grandma seems to inspire Elsie to get up. She places her empty glass of orange juice on a tray one of the white-gloved men presents her with and she starts to walk around, shyly, her hands behind her back as if she were hiding something.

She finds herself listening to the various conversations that fill up the room. She looks at Sylvia who smiles at her and waves hello, hello.

Elsie is now in the close vicinity of two women who look as if they're wearing the same clothes, although they're not. She hears one of the women pronounce Mother's name, and this makes her feel as if Mother is in the room with her; it makes Elsie happy.

One of the women, who is wearing a furiously red shirt with black polka dots and matching red lipstick, says something like, I know, it's been going on for some time now.

How long? the other woman with a white shirt and black polka dots asks.

I'm not sure. All I know is, it's very serious and Robert knows about it.

This intrigues Elsie. Robert is her father. What are these women talking about? Are they talking about her father? And if they are, what does her father know about? What's very serious?

He knows? the woman in red almost shouts.

Yes. Not only does he know but if you shout just a little bit louder, you'll catch the attention of the man in question. So for crying out loud, Lizzie, please, let's keep this down.

Elsie clutches her hands tighter behind her back. She suddenly feels very confused. First of all, why did the woman speak about crying out loud, since no one is crying?

Then, what man are they talking about, and what does another man have to do with her family?

Elsie moves just a little bit closer. This is exciting. She's about to uncover a secret, like in those detective movies Mother doesn't let her watch, although Sylvia does when her parents aren't around.

The woman in white suddenly grabs her friend's arm. It's him, she says, he's coming our way. His name is Olivier Sarnel. He's French and he's Sophie's father. Extremely attractive man, if you ask me. Heard he's very rich, too.

He looks just like Robert, the woman in red says. No wonder Leora fell for him.

Elsie finds herself face to face with the man in question, who indeed looks like her father. Now she is even more confused. And when the man extends a hand towards her and says, you must be Elsie, she doesn't quite know what to say.

How do you know I'm Elsie? she asks defensively.

Because you look just like your mother and because you are my daughter Sophie's friend.

The man has a strange accent. He smells of cigarettes and his eyes are blue like the ocean.

Elsie feels her cheeks turn red. How do you know my mother? she asks him.

I met her at a school meeting, he says smiling warmly. Elsie feels reassured, although she doesn't know why.

Those two women were saying all these things about my mother, Elsie says, pointing to the two different polka dots, who immediately seem to crease into themselves.

Who are you, little girl? the woman in red asks nervously.

Elsie hates being called a little girl, so she answers as coldly as she can, I'm not a little girl and my name is Elsie Posner. Who are you?

The two women tell her they're her mother's friends, then they look at each other in a concerned way and walk away, speaking in loud whispers.

The man with the blue eyes laughs and tells Elsie he hopes she doesn't believe any of the things those women were saying.

They're nincompoops, aren't they? Elsie asks the man, who doesn't seem to understand her question but who answers yes anyway.

As Elsie goes on talking with the man, whom she finds very kind, Bubbles Mayham rushes over to her and tells her that Sylvia is waiting for her and it is time for her to leave.

Why? Elsie asks, surprised, because after all, it isn't that late yet.

Because your mother wants you home before five. Now, let's go get your coat, here comes Sylvia, hello, Sylvia, how are you, I'm fine thank you and I think it's time for this young girl to go home, yes, yes, I know (Elsie notices that Bubbles is looking at Sylvia in an unusual way, as if she were trying to tell her something else). Now here we go, bye-bye sweetheart, send my love to your mother, no you don't need to say goodbye to the man, now go, *go*, or you'll be late.

As they are walking out the door, Elsie asks Sylvia why Bubbles Mayham looked so nervous.

What do I know, these rich people, they're all crazy, Sylvia mumbles. Let's go home.

As they sit in the taxi, Elsie thinks about what she

heard the two women say about her mother and Sophie's father. Somewhere, the words make her uncomfortable, as though they are an itch she cannot scratch.

When she arrives home and Mother has given her a big hug, she asks her if she knows Sophie's father.

Why do you ask? Mother asks, surprised.

Because he said he knew you, Elsie answers.

Mother answers something like that's nice, why don't you come say hello to your father?

As she turns around to follow her mother, Elsie sees that Father has been standing there all along and his face looks very red. He reaches his big hand out towards Elsie's and gives her a kiss on the cheek. This time, the kiss feels warm, like a pillow that's been slept on, and she can feel it against her cheek for moments afterwards.

That evening, the phone rings incessantly and Elsie wonders if Mother and Father are organizing a party, because that's when the phone usually rings that much.

When Mother comes to kiss her goodnight, Elsie asks her if they're organizing a party.

No sweetheart, we're not, she says. Go to sleep now, you've had a long day. And she kisses her on her forehead, a long and wet kiss.

Later that night, Elsie hears the phone ring again and she thinks she hears some cries as well, but her thoughts are too blurry. As she feels herself sink back into sleep she hears the front door slam abruptly and it reminds her of the day they closed the coffin of her aunt Barbara and the noise resonates in her ears for a long time.

The Ladies

They decided to play ladies at dusk. Little Mandy would be Mrs Tackaway, big Lauren would be Mrs Dunlop. They quickly got out the lounge chairs from the garage, shook the dust off them and ran back to the lawn, panting, their bodies overwhelmed by the weight of the chairs.

'Quickly, go get the nail polish,' said big Lauren. 'We still have time before they change for supper. It's in my mother's bedroom, in the bottom-left drawer of her dressing table. Get the one called "Pearliest Pink".'

Little Mandy ran off, all excited. Big Lauren set up the lounge chairs, took off her shorts and T-shirt and stuffed a pair of socks into her one-piece bathing suit, in an attempt to fake big breasts. From afar she looked almost like a young girl with fully developed breasts, but close-up it was all too easy to tell she was a girl, no more than ten years old, with dark blue eyes and a tanned complexion. She had a long, thin body and was very tall for her age. Her hair was short and curly and made her look slightly like a tomboy. But when she smiled, her white teeth sparkling and her two deep dimples echoing that smile, her femininity could not be mistaken.

She lay down in the chair and closed her eyes. It was starting to get chilly, but she was determined to stay out there until the end of the game. She could hear the waves crashing on to the rocks, the squall of the seagulls tearing through the sky, the rustling of the trees. She could also hear the grown-ups talking and laughing. She thought it strange, the way grown-ups respond to something funny. 'They all start laughing at the same time,' she thought to herself, 'and then they're all silent at the same time.' It sounded almost like the ripple of the waves, coming and going incessantly. Then she heard someone laugh very loudly and she recognized her mother's voice. This time she was laughing alone and no one was joining in.

She opened her eyes and saw the sky had become a glorious pink. At the same moment Little Mandy came back with the nail polish. She was six years old, with long wavy blonde hair. Her brother Eric, whom she was very fond of, was eleven years old; this summer, he was away at horse-riding camp and Little Mandy missed him.

Little Mandy was always very neatly dressed in lace dresses and frilly tops. She was fond of big Lauren, whom she had seen for the last three summers since both families rented houses in the beach town of Arcachon, in France. This summer, though, both families were sharing one big house together since Patricia's husband Jerry was away.

Little Mandy's mother Lana was an attractive and energetic woman, with auburn hair, light brown eyes and tight thin lips. Her husband Thierry was a successful lawyer who spent lots of time walking around the house smoking large cigars and talking on his cordless telephone with a preoccupied look on his face.

Big Lauren's mother Patricia was a thin and pale woman who always looked depressed and who, according to the latest rumours, had lately become addicted to potent tranquillizers. She wore an unusual amount of make-up and had recently taken to the bottle, a habit she didn't bother concealing from anybody, a call for help which, perhaps because of its conspicuousness, went unnoticed for too long a time.

Patricia's husband Jerry was an important film producer and spent most of his time abroad. Patricia and he had been on the verge of separating for a long time but, despite their numerous quarrels, still remained together, mostly for the sake of their daughter, whom they tried to shield from the grim reality of the situation.

'Okay, Mrs Tackaway,' said big Lauren, 'it is time we applied the polish, don't you think?'

'Oh, yes!' squealed Little Mandy.

Both girls started applying the bright pink nail polish to their toenails. It kept streaming on to their skin and by the time they started to wipe off the residue it was already too late: the nail polish was stuck.

'Oh well,' sighed big Lauren, 'it still looks nice, doesn't it? I don't know how Mother puts it on, it never looks like this. With her it's always neat.'

She turned her head towards Little Mandy, suddenly her eyes shone with excitement. 'Guess what I stole from my mother's bag this morning?'

'Stole?' exclaimed Little Mandy. 'What d'you steal? Lemme see!'

Big Lauren pulled out a lipstick from her shorts' pocket.

'What's it called?' asked Little Mandy. They both bent their heads down to look at the name of the lipstick.

'Flabbergasting Flamingo,' big Lauren read slowly.

'What's that mean?' enquired Little Mandy.

'Here, I'll put it on for you. Open your mouth.'

She smeared the lipstick on to Little Mandy's lips, then applied it to her own, her eyes closed.

'Wow!' exclaimed Little Mandy, bewildered. 'How d'you do that?'

'Practise,' answered big Lauren casually. 'Stood in front of my mother's mirror and practised.'

'Wow,' repeated Little Mandy.

Now that they both had their make-up on, they felt ready. Although Little Mandy envied big Lauren's breasts, they found no alternative for her. The only thing they did come up with was big Lauren's T-shirt, but it was too bulky to stick under another shirt, so Little Mandy did without. They sank into their chairs, this time for good. The only new problem was that night was approaching fast. Soon it would be dark and the grown-ups would call them in for supper.

'Well, Mrs Tackaway,' said big Lauren, clearing her throat and crossing her legs, 'what have you been up to lately? Hold on, let me get my cigarette.'

She picked a twig from the grass, wiped it, and stuck it in her mouth.

'Would you also like a cigarette, Mrs Tackaway?'

'Oh, no, thank you,' said Little Mandy.

'It has been such a long time since I've seen you, my dear, yes, indeed. What have you done this week?'

'Well, Mrs Dunlop,' said Little Mandy, beaming, 'last Tuesday I went to the hairdresser, Wednesday I went shopping, Thursday I had dinner with my grandma, and Friday I had a baby.'

'Not "grandma", stupid,' said big Lauren in a stern

whisper. 'A lady doesn't call her grandmother "grandma". Besides, a lady doesn't want to spend time with her grandmother. It's boring. Say you had the Brownings over for dinner.'

'Oh,' answered Little Mandy slightly flustered. 'Well, Thursday I had the Brownings over for dinner and Friday I had a baby.'

'Oh, really,' answered big Lauren, with a fake puff on her twig. Then she paused, uncertain as to what to say next about the baby. So she just asked Little Mandy what its name was.

'Thierry,' she answered.

'I see,' replied big Lauren thoughtfully.

Then they were quiet for a while. Little Mandy was getting cold but she didn't dare tell big Lauren, who in turn was freezing since she wasn't wearing anything besides a bathing suit.

'Aren't you cold, Mrs Dunlop?' asked Little Mandy in a trembling voice.

'But of course not,' answered big Lauren. 'How can I be cold in such beautiful weather?'

'But it's dark out!' cried Little Mandy. 'Soon it will be black and Mummy and Daddy will come looking for us!'

'We are old enough not to need mummies and daddies. We are ladies, Mrs Tackaway, do not forget.'

Little Mandy grew silent. She wanted to cry but held back her tears.

'Mrs Tackaway, wasn't that you I saw at the Brensons' the other night? You were wearing such a lovely green dress. And your husband, what a charming man ... how old is he?'

'Oh . . . sixteen,' said Little Mandy proudly. 'He bought me the dress,' she added, blushing.

'Well, well, what a nice husband you have,' said big Lauren, pulling her T-shirt over her head as quickly as possible. 'My husband buys me pearls and diamonds every day.'

'So does mine!' cried Little Mandy.

'And not only does he buy me pearls and diamonds, but he buys me houses and ponies too. And he's twenty years old.'

'Your husband is not as nice as my husband. My husband is nicer. He gives me kisses every day,' Little Mandy said defiantly.

Big Lauren remained silent. In the background, they could hear their parents preparing dinner, the sound of the dishes resounding above the crashing of the waves.

'Where are the girls?' Little Mandy heard her mother ask. She was about to answer when big Lauren put her hand on her mouth.

'Shut up,' she said.

Little Mandy, frightened, pushed her hand away. She felt tears stream down her cheeks and hid them stoically. Then she told big Lauren that she wanted to go home.

'Not now,' said big Lauren. 'Soon, but not now. Tell me more about your baby. Do you take care of him alone or do you have someone to help you?'

'Oh, both,' she said, wiping her tears.

'What do you mean, both?'

'I help, and Mercedes comes and helps.'

'I see. Well, Mrs Tackaway, that's good to know because I'm desperately looking for help, the house is such a mess,' said big Lauren, her voice taking on a surprisingly older tone. 'What does your husband do?'

'My husband?' Little Mandy whispered to big Lauren. 'I don't know what he does.' Then her eyes lit up suddenly and she said, 'He sells oil in Saudi Arabia.'

Big Lauren looked at her surprised. 'That's nice,' she said. 'He must be rich.'

'Oh, yes,' answered Little Mandy, 'he's very rich.' She cleared her throat as she said so. 'What does yours do?' she asked after a while.

'He's a banker. But he's also a doctor.'

Little Mandy didn't answer.

'Would you like to go look at department stores tomorrow?' asked big Lauren. 'My husband and I are going shopping after lunch.'

At the same moment, they heard the grown-ups calling them. 'Mandy! Lauren! Where are you?'

This time Little Mandy jumped out of her chair, but big Lauren grabbed her by the arm.

'Don't, Mandy, let's not go yet, let's play a Little more. I like this game, come on,' she pleaded, in a near desperate voice.

'Don't grab my arm like that, it hurts,' Little Mandy whined. 'And I don't want to play any more. I'm cold and I want to go home . . .'

'Oh, come on, Mrs Tackaway, ladies do not say they suffer, they have to endure all.'

'They have to what?' Little Mandy asked, distracted by her friend's sophisticated vocabulary.

'Endure. Don't you know what endure means, Mrs Tackaway? You must endure your husband, you know.'

'Oh, yes,' Little Mandy said, a lost look on her face. 'But, Mrs Dunlop, let's go home now.'

'Not yet,' big Lauren murmured. 'Please, not yet.'

'I'm going home. I'm hungry, I'm cold and I want to see my mummy.'

'You want to see your mummy? At your age, Mrs Tackaway? Tss tss . . .'

'I'm not Mrs Tackaway, I'm Mandy! And you're Lauren and you're a mean girl and so is your husband and I'll tell on you!'

'You'll tell on me! A lady your age! With a baby and a husband! I think you are past the age of telling on people, Mrs Tackaway,' she said in a disapproving voice.

'Come on, Lauren, let's stop playing. I want to go home. I'm cold. We can play again tomorrow!' she said in a small, helpless voice.

'I said no. I'm older and you must listen to me or else I'll hit you.'

'But why?' Little Mandy asked incredulously. 'Why would you hit me?' She started crying, while big Lauren remained motionless, gazing at her with a blank look on her face.

'Ladies don't cry,' she finally said.

At that point Little Mandy started to make a run for the house but big Lauren caught up with her.

'Let me go!' Little Mandy shouted. 'Please, let me go! Mummy! Daddy! Come help me!'

She started screaming at such a high pitch big Lauren kicked her in the shins, probably harder than she meant to. 'Shut up,' she said after she saw her fall to the ground in pain. 'Shut up or I'll kick you again.'

Little Mandy pulled up her skirt in bewilderment and saw a patch of blood on her left leg. She stopped crying and looked at big Lauren, who this time looked uneasy.

'It's nothing,' she said, not quite convincingly. 'Put some alcohol on it and it will heal right away.'

'If you think my daddy won't see this, you're wrong. Not only that, but I'll tell him you wanted to kick me again, and you'll see what will happen to you,' said Little Mandy in a low, threatening voice.

'Well, why don't you just go ahead, you Little snot?' asked big Lauren, slightly uncomfortably.

'Oh, don't you worry,' said Little Mandy, shaking her finger at her. 'Don't you worry, you snot yourself.' Then she became pale at the thought of what big Lauren might do to her next.

'And don't you worry that I'll tell my father what you did,' said big Lauren.

'But what did I do?' asked Little Mandy, in genuine surprise. 'Besides,' she added in a low voice, 'I don't know when you would tell your daddy, since he's never here anyway, and—'

'That's a lie!' shouted big Lauren. 'That's a real lie! My daddy calls me, my daddy works very hard, not like yours who walks around with a telephone all day long and his cigars, at least, my daddy, he takes real care of me when he's here—'

'Well, so does mine!' cried Little Mandy.

'Okay, Mrs Tackaway, there's no time for all of this right now,' said big Lauren in a new tone of voice.

'But the game is finished! You can't go on with it any more!' Little Mandy cried.

21

'Do you remember what I told you before?'

'What?' asked Little Mandy, trembling.

'I told you if you don't shut up, I'll kick you again.'

'You're not Lauren any more. You're not my friend any more,' said Little Mandy, her voice quivering with fear.

Big Lauren didn't answer. She just paced around, an angry look on her face.

Suddenly Little Mandy sprang up and, despite the pain in her right leg, managed to run away before big Lauren could catch up with her.

'Mummy! Daddy! Help me!' she screamed as she ran. By that time, she was close enough to the house for her parents to hear her, and big Lauren, unable to pursue the game, threw herself into the wet grass, crying.

'What in the world is going on here?' Lana said, as she ran towards her daughter, frightened. 'Have you been hurt, darling?'

Little Mandy showed her bleeding leg and pointed towards big Lauren's body on the grass, a mass of weeping matter, whose sobs pierced through the still of the night.

'Lauren could *not* have done that,' Lana said reproachfully, as she held her daughter in her arms. 'Come, my sweet, let's go get Tricia. And you, Lauren, why don't you come into the house with us. I'm sure your mother will want to talk to you. And not only that, but dinner is ready and both of you must be starving.'

Big Lauren shook her head and remained motionless.

'Lauren, I am not your mother, but I do think it would be wiser if you came back in with us. Besides, you're going to catch cold out here. Come on, don't act like a child.'

Big Lauren still didn't move. On the contrary, she dug

her face deeper into the grass. 'Fine,' said Lana, 'stay there.' The phone started ringing and someone picked it up after the third ring. As they walked back, Little Mandy could distinguish Patricia's shadow through the window, holding a long cigarette in one hand and the phone clutched to her ear in the other.

Lana carried her daughter halfway to the house but had to let her go after a while since she was too heavy.

'C'est quoi tout ce bouquant?' asked Thierry, as he walked towards them, a glass of Scotch in his hands.

'What is "bouquant", darling?' Lana asked in her husky voice.

'It's slang for noise,' answered Thierry. 'I was asking you what the hell all this noise was about. What happened to your leg?' he asked Little Mandy, as he suddenly caught sight of the blood. 'And what's this lipstick on your lips?'

'We were playing ladies and then Lauren kicked me,' she whimpered.

He grabbed her leg in order to look at it, gave his glass of Scotch to his wife, who took a loud slurp from it, and carried his daughter back to the house where he took care of her, more attentive than he'd been for a long time.

'Believe me, Amanda,' he said, applying some alcohol to her wound, 'if I didn't have to come here every year, I wouldn't. I'm sick of this other family here: always having to see them, always having to drink with them, eat with them and now live with them, bon Dieu, and when the husband is here, celui-là alors quelle histoire, with the coucou wife, you know, of course, that she's a little bit coucou, Lauren's maman, with all the booze and—'

He stopped abruptly, aware that he might be talking

too much in front of a six-year-old. 'Well, she's not really coucou, just a little bit crazy, that's all, not too much though, almost as much as your mother. Let me tell you, both of them together—'

'Mummy's not crazy!' Little Mandy gasped.

'Did I say she was crazy, okay, okay, stop moving your leg. What is all this dried nail polish around your feet? Playing with your mother's make-up again?' He smiled at her, then winked as she blushed and couldn't help herself from smiling as well. 'Well, here's a nice bandage. Enough. Just be careful when you go play with that girl Lauren. One never knows what she might do next, just like her mother. Why did she kick you anyway?'

'Because I didn't want to play with her any more,' Little Mandy said, lowering her eyes and making herself look as vulnerable as possible. 'And then she said if I didn't shut up, she would kick me again.'

'She said that? What a little brat. If I were her father . . .' he mumbled underneath his breath.

'What?'

'Nothing. Ah la la, ces gosses alors . . . Go see Maman, go. I have to make an urgent phone call.'

He kissed his daughter and closed the door as she walked away, wearing her new bandage like a trophy. On her way to the kitchen, she heard her mother talking to Patricia. Instead of entering the kitchen right away, she decided to hide in a little alcove right behind the door, which once served as the house's main junk closet. It still retained the strong odour of various detergents and moth-balls, and some old newspapers were scattered around the floor, their yellow sheets worn out with time.

In the right-hand corner of the alcove was a hole, large enough for two people to watch through. That hole led directly into the kitchen and enabled anyone to spy on whoever they wished. Big Lauren had discovered the hole two summers back and, since then, both girls had used it quite consistently, without ever being caught. They called it 'the web', since a big spider's web hung there permanently.

Little Mandy crouched in the corner, her knees up against her chin, and listened attentively, her eyes pressed against the hole as she watched both women, their heads almost pressed together, each of them holding a glass of brownish looking liquor.

'She can't go on like this,' Lana was saying. 'You have a wonderful daughter, but I think she's a little too ... How shall I put it, a little too ... Well, frankly, Tricia, too violent. Now, of course, it might be that she's repressing a whole bunch of painful things, such as your relationship with Jerry, her relationship with Jerry, for Christsake, she hardly ever sees her father, but whatever the real reason may be, she just can't go on kicking people because they won't play with her. You must teach her that. Mandy is younger than her, more vulnerable than her and you know how much she loves her. But Lauren cannot take out her anger on Mandy—'

'Well, who is she going to take it out on?' Patricia interrupted brusquely. 'She can't take it out on me. I'm a wreck and I take enough out on her, poor thing—'

'Yes, I know. And that may be the problem. She's not your confidante, Tricia. She's your daughter. Your ten-year-old daughter. Why don't you go out and talk to her,

Tricia, tell her you understand her anger, explain to her what she did wrong? . . . She's lying out there in the garden, her head in the wet grass. She won't come into the house.'

'I don't know how to talk to children. I'm a lousy mother and Lauren knows it. I'm the child in the family. I'm the one who needs comfort.'

'You're a great mother, Patricia,' Lana said in a soothing voice. 'And you've got to stop beating yourself up like that all the time. Come. Let's go out together and talk to Lauren.'

Patricia shook her head gently and closed her eyes for an instant. 'I hate my life,' she said in a hoarse whisper.

Little Mandy noticed that her mother looked nervous. She saw her put her arm around Patricia who looked very pale. She flung back her long black hair, took out a compact, started applying some eyeshadow, then suddenly let the eye brush drop, bent her head down and began crying quietly.

'Tricia, what's the matter!' Lana exclaimed, bending over and taking her hand. 'I'm sorry if I was too blunt. I'm sure we can do something about all of this. Lauren *is* a wonderful girl, I mean it's only two kids, really—'

'Oh, it's not about that, Lana. I'm sorry that happened but it's not about that . . .'

'What is it about? Jerry?'

'Yes,' said Patricia, her eye make-up smeared all over her face, 'he called me just ten minutes ago and told me he won't be coming back for a while. Three months, maybe four. He said it's for a new film but I know he's lying. I know it. I'm almost positive I heard a woman in the background, laughing or something. Who knows who she is . . . I'm so sick of waiting for him . . . He said he wants Lauren to go and spend the rest of the summer with him. I don't know what to do.' She dried her tears, opened her compact once again and finished reapplying the eyeshadow to her eyelids, then snapped it shut and threw it into her handbag.

'I'd better go get Lauren now,' she said, sighing. 'I'm sorry about all of this. I really am. And you're right. She is suffering. She always asks when Daddy is coming home. I always lie and say very soon. Although it's not such a lie since it's more or less true, I never know when he's coming back. You see, Mandy is one of her only friends. She doesn't have an older brother like Mandy does. She doesn't have that many friends in school. I'm worried about her, Lana . . .'

She sat back down and took a deep breath. 'Sometimes life doesn't seem like it's worth it any more. Between her and me there hardly seems to be any room left for happiness. It's only when Jerry is here that things are different.'

She got up and brought a bottle to the table. 'More brandy?' she asked.

Lana shook her head.

'When Jerry's here,' she continued, 'everything is alive again. Full of fights, yes, but also full of love, sex – great sex we have, Jerry and I, when he's not out there in America fucking another woman . . .'

'Tricia,' Lana said, looking at her disapprovingly, 'you shouldn't drink, really, not with the girl crying out there. I mean, you've already had two drinks.'

'Don't tell me what to do.'

She drank the brandy in one shot. Little Mandy saw

the way her whole body seemed to relax afterwards, how Patricia seemed to let loose, like the Jell-O they had eaten last night, when it was raining.

Patricia stood up slowly and tried to smile at Lana, who shook her head as she looked at her. 'Tricia, dear, don't think about it right now. I'm sure everything will be fine. Really. Jerry will come back. I know it. He loves you too much to leave you.'

'You think so?' she asked in a wretched tone of voice.

'Yes, I think so. You'd better go see your daughter now, I'm sure she wants to talk to you. And I'd better go and look for mine and give her some supper.'

Patricia left the kitchen and Little Mandy waited a while before coming out of the alcove. As she was walking out, she heard a faint noise coming from the other side of the hallway and when she looked out she thought she saw big Lauren dashing out of there like lightning, her bare feet squeaking on the floor. But it was so sudden, she couldn't tell if she was imagining it or not. 'Maybe it's Mme Berthaud's daughter,' she said to herself, referring to the next-door neighbour who often came in to help clean the house and who had a daughter about the same age as Lauren.

'Here, have some food,' said her mother, without turning around, as she entered the kitchen. 'You haven't eaten anything all day.'

'I'm not hungry,' said Little Mandy.

'Okay, so don't eat.'

Little Mandy crossed her arms and sat down, vowing to sulk.

'Here's some cold chicken salad, some corn on the cob

and some cheese. I can't stay with you. I'm going to go see how Tricia is doing out there.'

Little Mandy didn't answer. She started picking at her food, then left it untouched. She could hear her father's voice on the telephone. She walked up to her bedroom and looked out of the window. It was cold and windy now. There was a full moon and the sound of the nearby owls resonated through the night air. As she started to get into her nightgown, she heard Patricia's voice calling, 'Lauren! Lauren!' Then, about ten minutes later, she heard other voices joining in, her mother's, her father's, followed by Mme Berthaud and M. Colin the electrician who happened to be at Mme Berthaud's house. She then heard her mother's footsteps, running up the stairs and knocking on her door.

'Lauren has disappeared,' she said, panting. 'Do you know where she could have gone?'

'No,' said Little Mandy. 'I don't.'

'Well then, do you want to come and help us look for her?'

'No, I don't,' she answered coldly.

'Okay. Never mind. But you must know, Mandy, that this is not a game any more. This is for real. We can't find her anywhere.'

'I know, but she was mean to me,' she said, sitting back on her bed.

'Okay, I have no time to argue with you. If you do want to help, go get Mme Berthaud, she'll be staying in the house until we get back. You can go out with her, she has a flashlight and, whatever you do, stay close to her. The woods are dark and big, you might get lost. I don't know exactly what happened between Lauren and you, but you should try to put it aside for now and come and help us find her. She is your friend, despite the fact that you quarrelled.'

'I don't care about Lauren any more. I don't care about what happens to her. She's not my friend any more. I don't like her any more. I hate her. I never want to see her again,' she said sulking, her legs swinging from the bed.

'Don't ever say, "I hate her," again,' said her mother, lifting her chin up and looking her straight in the eyes. 'It's a horrible thing to say about anybody. How would you like it if someone said such an ugly thing about you?'

'I wouldn't care.'

'Okay, Mandy, do as you wish. Play the stubborn Little girl. If you change your mind, go and get Mme Berthaud. She's downstairs watching television.'

'Goodnight, Mummy,' said Little Mandy softly.

Lana went down the stairs rapidly. Little Mandy got underneath the covers and for the next four or five hours, in between her sleep, she heard voices calling, 'Lauren! Lauren!' At times she opened her eyes and leaned out of the window, only to see flashlights and torches all around the woods and near the beach, until she fell asleep for good and didn't wake up again until dawn, when she heard police sirens breaking through the incessant sound of the waves, wailing desperately as a pink sun rose on the horizon.

The Yellow Slippers

The Mother told the daughter to stop crying. She said, at your age one doesn't cry like that. Stop crying like this, you're sixteen years old.

The daughter said, yes, I know, but I can't stop, it's beyond me. It's him, she said, him. He humiliated me.

Who's him? the Mother asked. And what did he do to you? And before you tell me, wipe your face, your tears are all over the place. The daughter wiped her face and as she did so tears sprang out of her eyes again, a little angry fountain, and they landed on her shirt leaving a wet stain on the collar.

The Mother had her back turned to her. She was moving her body gracefully, from left to right, then right to left. She was preparing an apple pie for that evening, and every now and then she'd lick some apple filling off her fingers. I'm listening, she said, go on, tell me.

The daughter put her hair into a ponytail, blew her nose loudly and settled more comfortably into the couch. Father and I were walking down the Boulevard St Germain, she said, her voice trembling a little, when I suddenly remembered I had to call Xavier.

Who's Xavier, asked the Mother, turning around.

Oh, just a guy in my class, the daughter answered, waving her hand brusquely in the air. Why are you making apple pie? she asked. You never make it any more. It's

Father's favourite. Who's coming for dinner? Any guests? I thought Father was busy tonight.

No one is coming for dinner. You know what I told you about boys, the Mother said.

No, what did you say?

Never mind. Go on, she said, turning towards the stove again.

I'm hungry, the daughter said. Well, anyway, so I was talking to Xavier when I turned around and saw these really nice shoes in a shop window. The shop is called Capri Chaussures. Do you know it?

No, answered the Mother.

They were very elegant and very original looking. After I hung up I went to look at them. They were even more beautiful close up. They were Indian looking, you know, kind of pointy, with a gold rim all around them and little stars around the sides. They were yellow, a pale yellow. I looked for Father but I couldn't find him. I wanted to try them on, but I didn't dare go into the shop without telling him. What if he came looking for me and couldn't find me? Don't you think that was responsible of me?

Very, answered the Mother.

So anyway, after yelling, Father, Father, and making a total fool of myself on the Boulevard St Germain—

Don't always worry about making a fool out of yourself, interrupted the Mother.

Well, whatever, so anyway, after that, *and* after walking from the Place St Germain to the Rue de l'Université looking for him, I decided forget it, I'm going in anyway. Don't forget to put in some cinnamon. So I went in. I tried them on and they fitted me perfectly. And they weren't too expensive.

How much? asked the Mother.

Two hundred and fifty francs. Isn't that a good price?

Not for shoes that sound more like slippers to me.

They were not slippers, they were shoes. Anyway, while I was trying them on, I saw Father through the window. He looked very angry, you know the way he looks when he gets angry – his eyes get icy blue, he gets this nervous twitch and he walks around in circles—

Don't remind me, said the Mother, smiling.

So I started to make signs at the window, Father, Father, I was mouthing through the glass pane, but he didn't see me because he was so angry, so I had to go into the street with my socks on. And the saleswoman, this old hag, shouted – Mademoiselle, mais que faites-vous, vous ne pouvez pas sortir comme ça, what does she care if I go out with no shoes on? Then Father saw me and came bursting into the shop. He started shouting at me in front of the saleswoman and the customers, then he looked at the shoes and he screamed: You really think I'm going to buy you those ridiculous things? Why do you always want to look like a clown? Do you know I've been looking for you for half an hour, one minute you're in a phone booth then you're not, you think I don't have better things to do than run around looking for you everywhere, Ah, ces jeunes alors! he said to the saleswoman, who then made the mistake of asking me if I was taking the shoes.

When she said that, he looked at her like she was crazy and he said, my daughter cannot afford to buy herself these shoes. I pay for my daughter. But I don't pay for just anything. And I'm certainly *not* going to buy her these stupid shoes. Then he grabbed me by the arm and said, Nathalie, we're leaving this shop immediately, thank you, Madame, au revoir. And when we were in the street he started yelling at me again. You think you don't have enough shoes, he said. You think you can just walk into any shop, like a lady, and decide you want something and buy it, just like that. You're only sixteen, Nathalie. You're certainly not going to start buying things for yourself every week. I am not a rich man. And even if I were, I wouldn't buy you everything you want. Just on principle.

When is the last time I bought something, I asked him, and he said, just last week you and your mother went to the Galeries Lafayette and bought those bathing suits. Isn't that enough?

Then I remembered that it's true, we did buy those bathing suits last week. By the way, I tried the striped one on for Sylvie and she said I looked like a model in it. So you see? I was right to pick that one out. It was much nicer than the blue dotted one you liked. Anyway, Father was still yelling at me in front of the shop, and all these people in there were talking about us, so I just started crying because I was so embarrassed. Then, suddenly, who do I see but Betsy Varet, leaning against a tree and watching us. She had probably been standing there the whole time and I hadn't even noticed her. It was even kind of weird the way she was standing there, as if she had known that we were there . . .

What do you mean it was weird? the Mother asked quickly.

34

Oh, I don't know, I mean she didn't really seem surprised to see us there, like it was no big deal. So when she saw Father yelling at me like that she said, 'Raphael,' in her hoarse voice and smiled at me with her big made-up mouth, and Father told her I was acting like a spoilt girl, I wanted to buy these silly shoes, and he pointed them out to her and she asked me, why on *earth* would I want to buy such things, they looked so much like slippers. Are you listening?

Yes, I am, replied the Mother, still turned towards the stove. Go on, I'm listening. Is it almost finished?

Why, are you getting bored?

No, I'm sorry, go on. Betsy Varet . . .

What? What about Betsy Varet? She's horrible, right?

Actually, yes, she is.

Both laughed, Mother and daughter, and the latter squirmed in her seat. When will the apple pie be ready? she asked.

Oh, not for a while, she answered. You know that Betsy's husband just died, don't you? asked the Mother.

No, I didn't know, answered the daughter. But it makes sense, though.

What do you mean? asked the Mother, a bit nervously, what do you mean it makes sense?

Oh, I don't know, the daughter said. She just looked pretty good, much prettier than she used to. She never liked her husband, isn't that true? That's what Marion told me. She said Betsy couldn't stand his guts.

Did Marion really tell you such a thing? I'm surprised . . . And I doubt she told you she couldn't stand his guts. That's not a very nice way of talking. You can say they didn't get along. That's enough. We don't need to know more.

Whatever, said the daughter, flinging her hair back.

So she really looked that good? the Mother asked quickly. How did she look?

Oh, I don't know. She was wearing nice clothes and everything. Nice make-up. Actually, I started to think that I should wear lipstick. Like red lipstick. I mean not too red but, you know, bright enough. Sylvie always wears tons of lipstick. It looks great on her. Do you think it could look good on me?

I don't know, the Mother answered, her voice suddenly dropping lower.

What's the matter? the daughter asked, did I say something wrong?

No. Nothing's wrong. Now, go on with your story. What happened after that, after you bumped into Betsy Varet?

It smells good. Well, after Betsy said that thing about them looking like slippers, Father said, yes, that's so true they look just like slippers, ha, ha, ha, he laughed, were you like that at her age, Betsy? And they both started laughing. I don't know what they found so funny. Then I asked Father, very timidly, if he was sure I couldn't buy those shoes. He was silent, he looked at me and then, suddenly, he slapped me. That's it. That's the story. He slapped me in front of that stupid woman and in front of those same people in the shop. Then I ran away, very fast, without turning around. I heard him shout, Nathalie, Nathalie! Then I took the Métro, still crying, and then I came home. That's it.

Well, said the Mother, her voice trembling a little, I

don't know what to tell you. It's true that you shouldn't be so spoilt, but on the other hand I don't understand why your father got so upset ... I mean, I do but I don't. I mean trying on a pair of shoes is certainly not the end of the world. It's true that we're not rich. We're not poor, that's for sure, but we're not rich either.

Oh, really, said the daughter sarcastically. So what's this then, she said pointing towards the large white living room, with contemporary art hanging on the walls and lots of books everywhere. Oh, really, she said again, pointing towards the Louis XV chairs and the antique mahogany table. Well, if you want to know the truth, I think we're rich. I mean compared to the other people in my class, like Sylvie, we certainly are.

The Mother smiled, then she said, Nathalie, darling, you shouldn't compare yourself to anybody. Just be thankful for what you have. If you want these shoes so badly, then we'll think about it a little more. But I don't think it's right.

What's not right! the daughter shouted. What's so wrong, I mean, it's not like I ask for something every day, you know! Anyway, what's the matter with both of you, you've been so strange lately, you never used to be like that with me. So fine, I won't get the shoes, she added angrily.

The phone rang. The daughter picked it up and dragged the cord into her bedroom. The Mother heard her daughter's voice through the door, she was laughing now, she sounded happier. Then the Mother wiped her hands on the tea towel, took off her apron, and adjusted the temperature of the oven. She then went to the bathroom and looked at herself in the mirror. She noticed she had new wrinkles under her eyes, wrinkles which bulged through her pale skin. Her green eyes had lost their colour; they looked washed-out, she thought. She noticed some more grey in her wavy black hair, and her once full lips looked thinner too. Could it be, she thought to herself, could it be that I'm getting old? Are men still interested in 43-year-old women, she asked herself again. Of course they are, she said out loud, looking at herself one more time in the mirror. Then she raised herself on tiptoe, just to catch a glimpse of her figure. She heard her daughter laugh again, an earnest, fresh laugh, and she felt like going into her room and hugging her. But then, as she was looking at herself in the mirror, she suddenly started crying. Oh my God, she said to herself. She sat down on a little stool in the bathroom and she kept repeating, oh my God, I'm alone. She covered her face with her hands. He's already gone, she said in a whisper, he's already gone and she doesn't even know. Every time the image of her daughter came back to her, she cried even more bitterly, and although she knew she was in the next room, she seemed to be very far away.

After a while she got up and splashed some cold water on her face. Then, she put on some powder and some lipstick. She sprayed on some perfume before grabbing her coat, and yelled at her daughter through the door, I'll be back in a half-hour, please watch the pie for me. Her daughter called out, okay, bye, Mother, and went on chatting on the phone. The Mother could see her feet sticking out from behind the door. They were moving back and forth gracefully, as she lay on her stomach, her long black hair falling on to her shoulders. Bye, said the Mother again, too low for her daughter to hear.

When she got downstairs, she quickly walked towards the Métro since the father had taken the car with him. She got off at the Mabillon station and walked towards the Boulevard St Germain. When she saw the shop she stopped, breathless. The yellow shoes were still in the shop window and they were just as the daughter had described them. She walked into the shop and asked the saleswoman, a nice-looking old lady with white hair, if she had a size 37 left. The saleswoman said, I think we might, I'm not sure though, let me go look. She came back up almost immediately and said, I'm sorry, we just sold the last pair. Would you like to try on another size? The Mother said, no thank you, you see it's not for me, it's for my daughter, she was in here earlier this afternoon, I guess her father got very angry at her in the shop, and—

Oh, you're her mother! the saleswoman chuckled. My goodness this is funny! You should be glad you weren't here! Angry is not the word! He was fuming! I mean I know it's none of my business or anything but I don't think he should have yelled at her like that. Such a pretty girl. So pretty and sweet. Anyway, the funny thing is after he was done yelling at her and after he had slapped her – well, you know, she added, we all saw it through the shop window – well after that he looked really sad. His face took on a very sad expression, if you know what I mean.

Yes, I know what you mean, the Mother said, nodding her head.

Since he looked so sad, the saleswoman continued, the woman he was with looked like she was trying to comfort him or something – the saleswoman paused and blushed – I mean not really comfort him but, you know, she must have asked him what the matter was and everything. The saleswoman cleared her throat nervously. Then, he came back into the shop and said, where are those stupid-looking shoes my daughter wanted, those yellow slippers, and I told him, excuse me, sir, these are not stupid shoes, these are fine Italian shoes, and they're not slippers. I mean, Madame, I know he's your husband and everything, but really, you know, this is not a junk shop, I just had to tell him, we only sell the best quality here. So anyway, he took the shoes, he paid for them, then on his way out we had to call him back in because he had forgotten his change. Then he left very quickly. I'm surprised he didn't forget the shoes, the saleswoman added, laughing, really he was so nervous. Well, he's probably home by now, and he's probably already given them to her.

I see, said the Mother. Thank you. Goodbye.

She walked out of the shop in a daze. Outside, the sun was very hot. In one month, the daughter would start her summer vacation. She would kiss her parents goodbye one morning and leave for three weeks or a month, calling once in a while to say she was having a great time at her friend's house. When she had hung up, the Mother would experience that queasy feeling she always felt when she heard her daughter's voice from far away. Usually, she and the father would reminisce about her and look at old baby photographs, especially the one where she stood naked in a plastic swimming pool, a little blue hat on her head and a red balloon in her hand.

The Mother knew that this summer, she would be looking at the photograph alone.

Walking on Ice

'You've never looked so bad,' Netta told Adam. 'Your eyes got smaller, your stomach got bigger, your lips got thinner.'

'Thank you,' said Adam, reaching for a cigarette. 'Thank you so much.'

'Don't move,' said Netta. 'I almost got you right this time.'

She wore an old pair of jeans and a torn sweatshirt. In one hand she held a paintbrush, in the other she clutched the palette, a look of deep concentration on her face as she brushed the canvas scrupulously, moving her head gently with the rhythm of the music playing in the background.

'I'm sorry,' said Netta, 'I know it's a horrible thing to say, but it's true. You don't look as good as you used to.'

'Well, did you ever think that it might have something to do with you?' asked Adam. 'Did you ever think that you might make me feel like a piece of shit?'

'No,' said Netta, pausing in order to put her hair up. She had blue slanted eyes, dark wavy hair and full lips. Once her hair was up in a clumsy bun it emphasized her cheekbones and made her eyes look big.

'It's a pity you're so beautiful,' said Adam staring at her, 'because you really are quite a bitch.'

'I am not a bitch,' said Netta. 'I'm just very honest, that's all. I tell you everything that's on my mind. For better or worse.'

'Actually, bitch is an understatement,' said Adam, drawing on his cigarette and looking out of the window. 'You're a conniving, cold, self-righteous, egotistical, selfish, despicable witch—'

'You moved again,' said Netta, 'you moved your head. Are you done?'

'Done with what?'

'With insulting me?'

'Yes, I'm done. I wouldn't want to waste my breath on you for too long.' He looked at her scornfully and ran his fingers over his two-day beard. He was of medium height, with long thin legs and broad shoulders. His angular face had a Modigliani look to it; a long pointy nose, large expressive eyes closely set together, uneven lips. His reddish hair was wild and bushy; it was said to be one of his redeeming features.

Netta put her brush down and kicked some tubes of paint that were lying on the floor. 'Fine. So don't waste your breath then,' she snapped. 'Anyway, I just realized I have an appointment in ten minutes, I have to get ready. You can move as much as you want now.'

Netta waited for him to ask where she was going but he didn't. He just got up and walked out of the room, slamming the door. She heard him open the refrigerator, singing to the music. She almost wanted to go into the kitchen to tell him she was sorry, but she didn't. She wanted to ask him how he could sing, how he could stand it, but she didn't. She went into the bedroom and changed into a short skirt and black shirt. She looked at herself in the mirror and noticed she had lost weight; she looked very thin. She sprayed some perfume on, put on some face powder and let her hair down again. Adam came into the bedroom, surprising her. He looked at her coldly and passed his hand through his thick curly hair.

'How long are we going to go on like this?' he asked finally. 'I mean, this is really ridiculous.'

'I don't know,' said Netta, sadly.

'What don't you know?' asked Adam.

'I don't know how long this is going to go on for.'

'Do you want it to go on? I mean that's the main question.'

He was talking faster now. 'Do you want us to continue fighting like this every day and break up, or do you want to try and change it?'

'It? What's it? You can't change an emotion. If we're feeling anger and contempt for each other, well, maybe we should let it out and not try to pretend we're happy and life is glorious.'

'Whoever tried to pretend life is glorious? I certainly didn't. Besides, are you so unhappy with me? Do you really feel such contempt for me? Do you hate me or what? Sometimes I really get the impression that you hate me.'

'I don't hate you.'

'Well, do you love me then?' He lowered his eyes slowly, and this sudden display of vulnerability irritated her.

'I don't know,' she said. 'I don't know if I love you, I don't know if I hate you, I don't know anything. All I know is I'm going through a crisis and I'm only going to be able to resolve it alone, without anyone bothering me.' She paused for a moment. 'Why don't you get a job?' she asked him aggressively. 'You've been out of work for a month now.'

'What does a job have to do with this? Besides, I have a job—'

'Please,' she sneered, 'working six months out of a whole year is not exactly what I call a job.'

'Well, do I have to remind you how much money I make when I work?'

'That's not an issue.'

'Oh, but yes, it is an issue,' he replied abrasively. 'You like it that I make money, don't you? You wouldn't want to be with someone poor, would you?' He moved closer to her, a smell of aftershave trailing after him.

She shrugged her shoulders. 'What are you provoking me for? What's the big deal anyway? So you make money. So what?'

'So nothing,' he answered, his eyes resting on hers, blankly.

'Listen,' Netta said nervously, 'I don't like this either. I don't like fighting with you. But it's totally beyond my control. I don't understand why it's happening, I don't understand why I'm doing this, it's very strange for me too. It's like I want to provoke you in a way . . .' She looked at her hands and tried to remove some red paint from her fingers.

'I think you need a shrink,' Adam said. 'Desperately. I don't think you're able to resolve anything alone. You've got too many hang-ups. Not only that, but I don't think you want to resolve anything at this point.'

'Yes, I do,' she said. 'I really do. Let me go now, I'm going to be late.'

'What kind of crisis is this anyway?'

'Please don't ask any questions, please don't. I don't want to upset you any more, I really don't,' she said.

He brought her towards him forcefully.

'Please, leave me alone, please . . .'

'Why can't we talk? Why can't we talk about this normally? Why are you being so difficult, so cruel?' He clutched her against him, her hair brushing against his face, the smell of paint emanating from her skin.

He put both hands around her waist and drew her to him gently. 'Come on,' he whispered to her, 'come on, let's stop fighting.' He tried to take off her shirt but she pushed him away.

'Don't,' she said weakly.

'I love you,' said Adam, pretending he hadn't heard her. 'I love you, I want you,' he said in one breath, trying to pull her shirt off again, to no avail.

'Stop it!' she screamed. 'Stop it! Please!' She pushed him against the wall, grabbed her handbag and ran out of the door, crying.

On her way down the stairs she ran into the upstairs neighbour, Mrs Fernstein, an elderly woman who always walked around in a flowered bathrobe. She said she was getting sick and tired of all this screaming, also, it'd been smelling of turpentine lately, and she knew it was coming from apartment 4a, where else would it come from, and surely she was aware of the policies of the building which she, Mrs Fernstein, had lived in for thirty-two years. This was a proper building with clean and decent hard-working people, she was sorry but she was just going to have to file a complaint against her, it'd been going on for too long.

Netta mumbled, 'Fine,' trying hard not to cry, and Mrs Fernstein followed her into the hallway. 'Fine?' she shouted, 'that's all you can say? Fine?'

'Listen,' said Netta, tears streaming from her eyes, 'I'm having a hard day. I'm sorry about all the screaming, I've just been having a hard time with my boyfriend. I promise it won't happen again. I promise. Do you hear me? I promise! I *promise!*'

She was shouting now, and Mrs Fernstein got frightened. 'Okay, okay, no need to shout, I'm not deaf. I believe you.'

Mrs Fernstein walked away mumbling to herself, leaving behind her the smell of a medicine cabinet.

Netta leaned against the hallway wall and sighed heavily. She pinched her lips very hard in order to stop herself from crying, and after a few minutes she left the building. It was a very warm day. The light was white and almost blinding, a reminder that summer was approaching. It seemed like more and more flowers were blossoming, adding colours and scents to the street.

When she arrived in the café, her friend Marta was sitting there, her dyed-blonde hair spiked up, heavy painted-glass earrings dangling from her ears. She was wearing a low-cut golden top, revealing her unusually freckled skin. She was talking to a rather unattractive man in his mid-forties. Netta was upset. She hadn't planned on seeing her with anyone else. She wanted to talk to her alone. She almost left the café but Marta saw her.

'Hi.' She waved at her. 'Meet Ted,' she said as Netta sat down. 'You've got a rip in your shirt,' she whispered to her.

'Hello,' said Netta coldly.

'Very pleased to meet you,' said Ted, shaking her hand. 'I was just talking to Marta here about her job. Fascinating. It's the first time I've met someone who makes jewellery. I love it. Just love it.'

'Oh,' said Netta.

'I mean these earrings she's wearing are just fabulous. Real works of art. I'll spread the word. Get you going. I mean, really.'

'That's very nice of you, Ted,' Marta said, her Spanish accent thicker than usual. 'Do you want some coffee?' she asked Netta. 'I'm going to have another cup. What's the matter with you anyway?' she added, looking at her. 'You look strange.'

'We've been fighting again,' said Netta. 'Can we talk?' she asked, lowering her voice.

'Not right now,' Marta replied, smiling sweetly to the man as he turned his attention back to her. 'Ted is on his way to Koala-Lumpur,' she said to Netta, almost proudly.

'Ku-a-la, not ko-a-la,' said Ted, pronouncing the syllables very carefully, slouching his body slightly to the left.

'Yes. Actually, Ted sounds like he's a great traveller. He's been everywhere. Haven't you?'

'I'm going,' said Netta abruptly, cutting Ted's answer short. 'Call me later. I need to talk to you alone.'

'I'm so sorry,' said Ted, standing up, 'I didn't realize . . .'

'That's fine,' said Netta, trying to smile, 'that's fine.'

'I'll call you later,' said Marta, looking at her in a concerned way.

She walked up 6th Avenue and turned left on Christopher

Street. She wondered why it was that Marta always went out with desperate, lonely men. It seemed that every month she met another man, usually middle-aged; the only men who had ever proposed marriage to Marta were the ones she deemed most unsuitable, a state of affairs which had eventually started to take its emotional toll. And in a selfish way, seeing her friend like that, as desperate as those lonely men, made her feel better about herself. Somehow, seeing someone more depressed than her relieved her of her own burden.

She stopped at a bakery and bought herself a little plum tart. As she approached 11th Street she realized she was afraid of facing Adam. She didn't know what to tell him. She didn't know what she wanted from him and wasn't sure he knew either. She couldn't go home. It had barely been a half-hour. What would she do at home? She didn't want to see him. She didn't think she loved him any more but didn't have the strength or the will to leave him. She was afraid of being alone.

She loved him.

She didn't love him.

She wanted him.

She didn't want him.

She hated his newly acquired belly and the way he slurped down beer.

He never used to drink beer.

She didn't desire him any more.

She didn't like the fact that his lips were icy and dry all the time. His kisses were cold as well.

She still loved the way he looked at her in the morning

when she first opened her eyes. She wondered how come he was always awake before her.

His eyes were grey in the morning and blue in the afternoon.

She enrolled at the School of Visual Arts and started taking painting classes in the graduate department. After a while she decided to switch from figurative to conceptual art. She started building a large sculpture out of plexiglas, wood and chicken wire. On the front of it she spray-painted a quote from Nietzsche: 'In the end one loves one's desire and not what is desired.'

The teacher, a bearded man in his late sixties, seemed doubtful. 'What about your still lifes? What message are you trying to convey here?'

'Who said I'm trying to convey a message?' she asked.

'We all end up conveying messages,' the teacher answered, 'whether we mean to or not, our work is always interpreted in a specific way.'

'Well, I'm trying to create a product here,' she said defiantly, 'not a statement.'

'Go ahead,' said the teacher, shrugging his shoulders and walking away.

She felt defeated. She looked around the room to see if any of the students had heard his comments, but apparently no one had.

She suddenly felt inadequate, angry at those who had seen so much promise in her: her mother, who had clasped her hands and gasped with admiration when she had seen her first painting, her high-school teacher who had taken her aside one day, to tell her that she had a lot of talent and should go to art school, and finally her college professor and college friends who came in large numbers to her opening, taking photographs of her (which were then published in the local paper), making her feel like a star.

What about all that awe and admiration? Was it unfounded? Had they all lied? She looked around the room. Many of the students seemed interesting, vibrant with energy. At one point three of them started laughing at the same time, their laughs echoing in the large, white room, making her shudder uncontrollably. She felt lonelier than she had been in a long time.

When she came home that night, there was a note on the refrigerator from Adam. It said that he was out with some friends, he'd probably be home late.

She made herself some pasta and watched the television screen blankly until Adam came home.

She opened her arms to him when she saw him. She let him kiss her avidly, the smell of liquor and smoke on his breath, his fingers caressing the back of her neck, awakening her to his touch, bringing her closer to him once again.

His lips were warm and soft that night.

She cut her hair short and dyed it jet black. She started wearing thick black eyeliner and antique clothing. She put four necklaces around her neck and wore bright red lipstick. Adam told her he didn't recognize her any more, her speech was different, her demeanour was different, even her laugh was different.

'What is this you're going through, a teenage crisis?' he asked her.

'I'm finding myself,' she said. 'I'm finding a new "me" I'm more comfortable with. To tell you the truth, I've never felt this good before.'

'You're deluding yourself,' said Adam, lying on the couch and looking at her, his arms crossed behind his head.

'I am *not* deluding myself,' said Netta. 'I mean do you always have to be so critical of me?'

'Listen,' said Adam, sitting up and stretching his long legs, 'you're twenty-five years old and you're suddenly going through a personality change. Don't you find that a little awkward?'

'Not at all,' she answered firmly, 'I don't think it's a question of age. Besides, do you realize how unhappy I was feeling? How mixed up?'

'Don't remind me,' he said sarcastically.

'Well,' she continued, ignoring his comment, 'ever since I started school, I've felt as though a new door has unlocked within me. It's a very nice feeling.'

'That's great,' said Adam, 'I hope it stays unlocked for a while.'

'Are you making fun of me?' Netta asked in a low voice.

'Not in the least,' he answered.

They looked uneasily at each other.

'What's the matter?' asked Netta nervously. 'Why aren't you saying anything?'

'What do you want me to say?'

'I don't know –' she shrugged her shoulders '– just something nice.'

'Okay.' He looked at her silently, his head cupped in his hands, his foot tapping on the ground.

'Why are you staring at me like that?' she asked, squirming in her seat. 'I mean, is it that hard to say something nice?'

'Sometimes it is, yes,' he answered, his gaze still fixed on her.

'Well forget it then,' she said, standing up, fidgeting with her necklaces.

'Come here, let me see your necklaces,' he said gently as she was about to leave the room.

She waited a moment before walking over to the couch. She sat down next to him and he carefully separated the necklaces one by one. 'These two are very nice,' he said, holding an African one and another with a large red stone attached to a thick silver chain. 'Is it coral?' he asked.

'I don't know.'

She wanted to hug him. She wanted to put her arms around his neck and kiss him. As she moved her head closer to his the phone rang.

'I've got to go,' he said after hanging up. 'I've just been offered a new job. It's an independent film production company; they pay very well.'

He was out the door five minutes later. 'I'll call you later!' he shouted.

She sat back down on the couch. She could still feel his presence, sitting by her, staring at her. A huge emptiness invaded her like a sudden gush of cold air, she could almost feel it slam against her face, forcefully, brutally.

'I hope it will be the same again,' she said out loud.

She started spending time with a group of people at school, mostly fellow students. She spent late hours with them in cafés or in bars, sometimes coming home drunk. Adam asked her if he could join them, he was interested in meeting her new friends. She said she preferred he didn't, at least not for now. She didn't give any further explanation.

She became active in various projects and spent many hours at school working on her sculpture. She'd often come home late at night, smelling of clay and glue, her fingernails dirty. She gave her sculpture the shape of an ice cube.

She tried to leave Adam several times. She'd pack her suitcase, put on her coat and would start crying before even making it to the door. 'I don't know why it's so difficult,' she'd sob, 'I guess it means that I still love you.'

'I guess so,' he'd answer, covering her wet face with kisses, beaming.

After a while, matters improved between Netta and Adam. She desired him once more, found herself anxiously waiting for him to come home at night. He started his new job, often took her out to dinner, bought her various gifts and one night he told her he wanted her to be his wife. It didn't have to be now but eventually. He stressed the word eventually. She told him she wasn't ready yet. He said he understood perfectly, they were still pretty young after all. Then he laughed and said he suddenly remembered all the horrible things they used to say to each other, he couldn't believe he had said all those things to her, and to think that was only two months ago. Nor could he forget the things she had said to him for that matter. He laughed again and slapped his hand on the table for emphasis. Netta replied that she didn't think it was funny, those moments were not easy for her, far from it, she didn't even want to remember them, they were too painful. Adam told her of course not, he didn't mean to joke about it. Netta asked him how he felt about being with her for so long, soon it would be four years, did he still feel the way he did in the beginning when they were so in love nothing else counted besides each other, they would sit around all day talking about the life they would have together, the number of children they wanted, the house in the country they would build with their own hands.

Adam smiled and answered that yes, of course he remembered, they were such idealists, it was almost amusing to think about it now. Netta asked him what was so amusing about it and he said the fact that they had such big dreams and so little drive. Netta agreed that it was paradoxical, but how did he feel about their relationship today, about the life they were currently leading. Adam said he had his share of worries about it, it was not always easy, but the good times far surpassed the bad times. She asked him if that was how he saw it, as good times versus bad times, if that was how he measured their relationship, as a balance.

He appeared hurt. He told her he could hear the familiar patronizing tone in her voice, he hadn't heard that one in a long time. She apologized and told him she didn't mean to be patronizing.

'What's wrong with seeing it that way, anyway?' he asked her.

'There's nothing wrong with it,' she answered, folding her napkin carefully. 'Forget what I said.' She felt a pang of remorse as she saw the expression on his face, his lower lip curling up as though he were about to cry, his eyes lowered to his plate.

She got up and kissed his forehead. It felt sweaty. She put her arms around his neck and tried to kiss him. He turned his head away.

'You always destroy things,' he said to her.

At the end of her first year in graduate school she met a man. He was a few years older than her, an attractive art historian who came to lecture several times on nineteenth-century art. He was tall, with thick black hair, bushy eyebrows and grave green eyes. His name was Julian. When she first heard him talk, she was intimidated by his eloquence and glowing self-confidence. But it didn't take her long to discover that underneath that exuberance lay a sensitivity quite similar to her own. He asked her out to lunch one day and she found herself unable to eat.

She went out to lunch with him on several occasions and by the end of the month she had lost five pounds.

She started dreaming about him. One morning she dreamt he was sitting on the front steps of her building, his chin in his hand, watching her. When she woke up she found Adam staring at her, like he always did.

'What were you dreaming of?' he asked her.

'Nothing, why?'

'You were smiling. In your sleep.'

Julian started telling her about his girlfriend. Her name was Helen, she was much older than him and lived in California.

They saw each other quite often, but not often enough. He missed her. He wished she could come and live with him in New York.

Netta didn't like the fact that he used his girlfriend's name in front of her; it created an intimacy with her she didn't want to have.

So she decided to be colder towards him. But the same dreams haunted her at night, destroying her mornings, leaving only the afternoons to forget about him.

One day, seated in a dark café, Julian looked at her and told her Helen had predicted that he would have an affair with someone else. Netta blushed and kept her head down, not wanting to respond, not knowing how to respond.

A few weeks later, he kissed her. She knew that everything would be different then, that what she had started again with Adam would be destroyed. That this time there would be no turning back. That this was what she had been looking for all along.

An excuse to leave Adam.

The will to leave Adam.

The strength needed to leave Adam.

She hadn't desired anyone like that in a long time. Every time Julian kissed her she felt her body warm up like an instant flame, burning inside her for hours on end, even when she climbed the stairs back to her cold apartment, to Adam who was waiting up for her, the television on, the lights on, his eyes closing despite himself. He never asked her where she had been. He seemed to take it for granted. And when she got under the covers, he still put his arms around her, whispering to her in his sleep, while she still felt Julian's lips against her skin, touching her imperceptibly, the sound of his voice resonating in her ears like a distant drumbeat.

She started spending time at Julian's apartment. Sometimes it was enough to just sit there quietly, her head on his lap, his hand caressing her hair. He told her more about Helen, she told him about Adam. Often he'd interrupt her in mid-sentence, kissing her languorously, telling her how much he liked her, how beautiful he thought she was. He also told her he felt very bad about Helen, he knew what he was doing wasn't right, he didn't know how long this could go on for.

Every time she left his apartment she felt as though she were leaving a moment of happiness behind. She'd linger on his doorstep, fumbling for words, her eyes betraying a sadness she desperately wanted to hide. 'Why do you look so sad?' he asked her once. She didn't answer. She couldn't answer. She couldn't tell him how increasingly difficult it was for her to go home after these secret meetings with him, leaving his arms only to find herself lying in bed next to Adam, reminiscing about her time with Julian, hoping for something she knew he wasn't ready to give her, and knew she wasn't ready to ask for.

She left Adam. She packed her bags one morning, knowing he wouldn't be back until the evening. She didn't want to face him. She left him a long note and signed it with a shaky signature. In the note she said she would contact him in a few days. She didn't mention Julian.

She stayed with Marta while she looked for an apartment. They stayed up late one night, talking until dawn, drinking tea.

'I'm going back to Madrid,' Marta said. 'I'm sick of the men in this city. I haven't fallen in love in over three years. I haven't even met anybody I remotely like.'

'What about Ted?'

'Oh, him . . .' she waved her hand disdainfully. 'He was very nice and very boring. It was a waste of time.'

Netta suddenly felt uncomfortable with her. Her desperation, her loneliness, her dirty apartment, all managed to make her feel even worse. She went to stay with some other friends of hers, an Italian couple who were both studying painting with her. She didn't see Julian during that time.

That same week, she found a small and bright studio in the East Village. She moved in immediately. She called Julian up and met him in a night-club. She found him at the bar. She wore high heels and a short skirt and he told her she looked very good. He asked her if she wanted a drink and she ordered a Scotch. As soon as she sat down at one of the nearby tables, he grabbed her and started kissing her. She realized that he was very drunk. 'I want to be mean to you,' he said suddenly, his hand underneath her shirt, kissing her neck.

She was struck by the sudden change in his voice, a brutality she had never suspected, which frightened her at the same time as it aroused her curiosity.

'You shouldn't like me so much,' he whispered in her ear. 'You shouldn't be with me. I'm a lush, a sadist, a jerk. I'm only going to hurt you.'

She ordered another drink. What was he trying to achieve by telling her this? She looked at him in disbelief. 'If you're trying to hurt me by saying this to me – well, it's not working,' she said.

He put his arm around her and said no it wasn't true, he was just provoking her, she was too beautiful, he couldn't be mean to her, although it was so tempting.

She asked him why. He said her fragility moved him in a strange sort of way. It made him want to break her. She stood up and said she had to leave, she didn't come here to hear things like that, besides she was not that easy to break.

He smiled and said of course not, and she felt like slapping him. He started kissing her again, told her she should stay, he wanted her to stay, he promised he wouldn't say mean things to her any more.

She stayed.

He brought her home at three in the morning but didn't come up with her. He left her by her front door, drunk. She felt dirty.

She called Adam up but he wasn't home. She wondered if he was with another girl. She missed him.

The next time she saw Julian, he apologized to her. 'I'm sorry,' he said, 'I was very drunk that night, I didn't behave correctly with you.'

'No, you didn't. Actually, your behaviour was almost pathetic.'

'Was it?' He appeared bothered.

She felt stronger, ready to confront the worst, ready to maintain her self-esteem. She was not going to let him break her.

'Was I really pathetic?' he asked her again.

'Yes,' she answered.

They spent the day walking around, hand in hand. He acted his usual way, stopping in the middle of the street to kiss her, joking with her, talking to her more intimately than he ever had.

They went up to her apartment and got drunk on a bottle of wine. They made love for the first time and lay quietly side by side afterwards.

'That was a disaster,' he said after a few minutes, gazing at the ceiling.

'Well, maybe next time it won't be such a disaster,' she said, trying to sound casual about it.

'I knew this whole thing would be a disaster from the beginning,' he said, turning towards her, staring at her naked body. 'We really should decide about this now. Either this is going to be a passionate love affair, or we should never see each other again. I really love my girl-friend, you know.'

'I know,' she said, wondering if he was telling the truth.

'No, you don't,' he answered.

'Okay, fine, so let's not see each other again,' she blurted out after a moment of silence.

'But I want to see you again.' He kissed her stomach, then her breasts. 'You break my heart,' he whispered to her, slowly bringing his body closer to hers. 'You break my heart, you little bitch.'

She pushed him away, pulled the sheet towards her and wrapped herself in it like a mummy, until only her face was sticking out. Then she started laughing. Uncontrollably. Hysterically. Julian tore the sheet off her and asked her what was so funny. She said she didn't know, she really didn't, it was just coming out for no reason, it must have been buried there for a long time. Julian squeezed her very hard against him and said he hoped she wasn't laughing at him. 'Don't be so paranoid,' Netta said to him. He attempted to smile, told her she was drunk, released her from his grip and left the bed.

She asked him where he was going and he said he was leaving. She remained motionless. 'Am I going to see you again?' she couldn't help herself from asking.

'I don't know. Maybe, maybe not.'

Before he left he kissed her goodbye, tenderly. 'I don't know why it is, but you bring out the worst in me. And at the same time I feel so attracted to you.'

'I think you're weird,' she said.

He shrugged his shoulders. 'Maybe,' he answered.

She wanted to ask him if he was that way with his girlfriend in California. She wondered what kind of a grip she had on him, what attracted him to her so much. Did she also bring out the worst in him? Or did she make him suffer?

'Does she make you suffer?' she asked him as he stood by the door.

'You're cute.' He smiled at her. 'I'll call you.'

Netta stayed in bed for several hours thinking about Julian.

Could she love him? she wondered.

Could he ever love her?

That night she called Adam up. When he heard her voice he hung up. She tried again but he didn't pick up. She tried every hour but she only got the answering machine, with the sound of Cat Stevens' voice on it, so at two in the morning she gave up and fell asleep instantly.

She told her friends about Julian. They all said he sounded dangerous. She told them she still had trouble taking him seriously, there was something just too clean about him. And when he provoked her, there was something very polished about his crudeness, very calculated, as if he were provoking himself as well as her; it was a game that they were meant to play together. And at this point, she wasn't sure how much she was willing to participate in it.

She saw him several more times. He was tender, considerate, passionate. At first she was cautious. But after a while she let herself go entirely. She reciprocated his tenderness, succumbed to his desires, opened herself up to him.

Adam seemed far away, a shadow in her memory. When she tried to picture his face she found herself unable to. He remained out of focus, like an old photograph dusty with time.

One day Julian stopped calling her. When she tried calling him he said he couldn't talk to her, he was back with Helen and wanted it to stay that way. He told her not to call again, it was useless, it wouldn't change anything, he was really sorry but he wasn't ready to be with two women at once and that was all there was to it. He hung up without saying goodbye.

She was unable to swallow anything for a week. She cried herself to sleep every night and cried when she woke up. She waited a few days before telling anyone what had happened. Her friends told her they weren't surprised, they had warned her about him, and lectured her for a few hours on how she needed to get a new grasp on life.

She spent more and more time working on her sculpture. She added plaster to it, clay, and stuck pieces of coloured chewing gum around it. It became so large and cluttered up that she had to move it to a different space.

The same teacher who had discouraged her about it came up to her and congratulated her. 'It's an interesting piece,' he said, 'more interesting than I thought it would be.' He smiled at her. 'You obviously have lots of things on your mind.'

She returned his smile, hoping he was not expecting her to answer. He remained motionless for a few seconds, cleared his throat and walked away.

As soon as he had his back turned, she started taking off everything: the plaster, the clay, the chicken wire, the wood, the coloured chewing gum, the Nietzsche quote. She stripped the sculpture bare, wiped its surface with a wet cloth and stood back to admire it.

It was perfect. A slick, hard and transparent ice cube. The light came through the plexiglas, a multicoloured rainbow which seemed to warm up the surface, giving it an almost surreal look.

Why hadn't she thought about it before? Why hadn't she left it bare from the beginning? She ran over to the teacher and asked him if he'd come and look at it again. She spoke breathlessly, her cheeks were flushed. He walked over with some other students, and they all gathered around it, speechless. The colours were streaming in from everywhere, it was almost blinding. 'God, this is amazing,' someone finally said. The teacher shook his head slowly, looked at Netta and told her he was impressed. 'Great work,' he said. 'Really great work.'

She went out to celebrate with a few other people from school. They went to a Mexican restaurant, ate nachos and drank lots of tequila. She felt radiant and happy. One of the students, Carlos, a sculptor from Bolivia, asked her for her phone number. She gave it to him.

Two days later, as she was drawing in her sketchbook, a woman she was slightly acquainted with came up to her and told her she had heard Julian was having his first book published, on the nineteenth-century French painter Paul Signac. Netta tried to appear nonchalant about it, but her trembling hands betrayed her.

'You really liked this guy, didn't you?' the woman observed.

'No, I didn't,' Netta replied scornfully.

She purposefully didn't buy his book. She read about it in various magazines, heard about it from different people. They posted photographs of him in the school hallways. She tore one of them off and brought it home with her. She sat on her bed and looked at it for a long time. His eyes, his smile, his hands, all looked somehow foreign to her. She tore the photograph into little pieces and threw it into the waste-paper basket. The phone rang. It was Carlos. She agreed to meet with him that same evening. As she relaxed in a hot bath, she remembered what her mother had told her one day, after the death of her father. 'You know,' she had said as they were drinking tea together, 'I'm always amazed by the fact that we all get over things. Even death. After a while, after all the suffering and the pain, life resumes its normal course. Differently, but it continues. It has to continue. You can't just give up, and you should always remember that. If one day you happen to suffer a great loss, or if someone hurts you terribly, you should just tell yourself that there will come a time when the pain, although it will never disappear, will lessen, and you'll be able to start over again.'

Her mother got over the death of her husband and remarried another man soon afterwards. She bore him a child and quit her job. But although she always appeared to be serene and happy, there was an underlying sadness about her that never went away. It grew with her as she got older. In the way she talked, the way she walked, the way she told stories, the way she laughed. She never mentioned Netta's father and kept all the photographs she had of him locked up in a drawer.

After her bath, Netta decided to take a nap. It was seven o'clock, two hours before her appointment with Carlos.

She didn't wake up until the next morning. She didn't hear the phone ring, or the three desperate messages Carlos left.

She never returned his calls. Eventually she saw him at school and apologized half-heartedly. He pretended he hadn't heard her and walked away rapidly.

She started getting used to living alone again. She decided to throw a house-warming party. Her friend Gia came over to help. They made thirty sandwiches and laid them carefully on a white platter next to the liquor bottles and the cheese and fruit. As she was preparing the food she looked at Gia. She suddenly wished Adam was there. He could be the one standing there, arranging the fruit in the basket, his eyes bluer than ever in the afternoon light. He would put his arms around her waist and kiss her neck. He would turn the music up and make her dance with him, waltzing around the living room, making fun of her clumsy steps, laughing and dancing with her until they were out of breath.

She tried calling him. A woman answered. She hung up, feeling like someone had just dug a big hole in her stomach.

'Let's cancel the party,' she told Gia, 'it was a bad idea from the beginning.'

'Oh, come on,' said Gia, stopping to look at her, 'you can't do that. People are going to be here soon. What's the matter anyway?' She put her hair up in a ponytail and put her glasses on.

'Nothing,' said Netta, her voice trembling a little, 'I just called Adam and a woman answered the phone, that's all. That means he's probably living with a new woman. I can't believe it . . . I'm in shock . . .'

'Well, what do you expect?' said Gia, coming over to sit next to her. 'You left him, didn't you? That's what you wanted at the time, and you shouldn't feel bad about it.'

'I know.' She sighed. 'But sometimes I wonder if I didn't make the biggest mistake of my life . . .'

'You didn't,' said Gia firmly. 'I can assure you, you didn't. You're only feeling this way because you realize that his life is going on without you, the same as your life is going on without him.'

'I miss him,' said Netta, feeling tears swell up in her

eyes. 'He was so good to me, never will I find another man who is so good to me.'

'Of course you will,' said Gia, putting her arm around her affectionately. 'Of course you will. Jesus Christ, I can't believe this is happening two hours before people are supposed to arrive. Are you going to be okay?'

Netta attempted to smile. 'No,' she said.

'Jesus Christ,' Gia said again. 'Just don't cry. Please don't cry. I don't know how to handle tears, they kind of make me nervous.'

'I won't cry,' said Netta. She got up and looked at herself in the mirror. Her hair was getting longer now, streaks of black were mixed in to her natural hair colour, she had big circles under her eyes.

'I look awful,' she said. 'I'm not ready for this at all. Just take a look at me.'

'You look fine,' said Gia without looking at her, rinsing some grapes and putting them in the basket. 'Go take a shower and you'll feel better.'

She followed Gia's advice. She wondered if she should have invited Adam, if she should have left a message with the woman. Would he have come? she wondered. Did he hate her after all she had done to him? He probably did. And with reason.

She let the water drip on her body for a long time, and when she went to greet her first guests, dressed in a tight black dress, high heels and a black hair turban, she felt as if that same wound within her had healed somewhat, although precariously; it was bound to burst open again at any time.

*

She bumped into Adam one afternoon. He was coming out of Balducci's, his arms full of packages. He tried to avoid her but she stopped him.

'Please, say hello to me, please,' she said, grabbing hold of his arm.

'Hello,' he said, pushing her arm away. 'I don't have time to talk. I'm in a hurry. Goodbye.'

'But you can't just walk away, you can't,' she cried, grabbing on to his arm again.

'Okay, so let me make myself clearer then. I don't want to talk to you. Got it? I don't want to see you. You bring back bad memories. Now please let me go.' His eyes sent little flashes of fury, his cheeks were bright red.

'If you only knew.' She sighed. 'If you only knew how much I've been thinking of you . . .'

'Yeah, right.' He smirked. 'That's why you took off one day like a goddamn coward and never gave a sign of life again.'

'I did give a sign of life. I called you. You hung up on me.' She paused and looked at him. His eyes were gazing upwards, watching a plane zoom by. 'How can you watch the sky at a moment like this,' she scolded.

'Precisely for that reason.'

'What reason?'

'Guess.'

'I loved you, Adam.'

'I'm in a rush,' he said. 'Goodbye.'

'Who's the woman you're living with now?'

'Oh, that's my new girlfriend, Samantha. Really nice girl. Very conscientious. Sensitive. She actually *cares* about things. Amazing. Not like you. You don't give a shit about anything. You never did.' He paused and grabbed some pears that were falling out of one of his shopping bags.

'So who are you fucking now?' he asked cynically. 'Or let me put it this way: did you leave me for another man, another victim, or did you leave because you were sick of me?'

'I wasn't sick of you. I left you because I felt I needed space.'

'I see. I suppose it would have been too much for you to tell me that directly.' His gaze softened for a brief moment.

'I also left you so that I wouldn't have to hurt you any more,' she added in a low voice.

'How generous of you. How kind. How good of you.'

He hailed a cab. 'See you one of these days!' he shouted. 'Or in another lifetime! Another planet!'

The cab rolled off before she could say anything. By her feet lay one of the pears, intact. She stepped on it violently, once, twice, until it was so crushed there was nothing more to step on.

Two weeks later, Julian appeared again. She opened the door to find him standing there, sheepishly holding a bouquet of white tulips.

'I made a mistake,' he said. 'I think I made a big mistake. I didn't behave well with you. I was kind of a jerk with you. Let's talk. Can I come in?'

She was in her bathrobe and had just washed her hair.

'No. Thanks for the confession but no. It's too late.'

She slammed the door on him and smiled to herself.

Was life going to treat her well from now on?

He rang the buzzer several times again but she ignored it. She hummed as she got dressed, and put on some make-up even though she wasn't planning on going anywhere.

He shouted from behind the door that he would be back, and she heard his footsteps sluggishly going down the stairs.

He came back the next day. He waited for her to come home from school. He pleaded.

'Please,' he said meekly, 'please, let me explain. Helen and I broke up, it's all over between us. Please, have dinner with me tonight.'

'I'm busy tonight. Goodbye, Julian.'

She slammed the front door in his face and walked up the stairs to her apartment with a renewed feeling of hope.

A few days later she let him in. She made him sit down and started screaming at him. She wasn't sure for how long. Ten minutes, maybe twenty. He stared at her incredulously as she poured her life out to him, screaming at him, insulting him, telling him how much she hated him.

She stopped as suddenly as she had started. She pushed her hair back violently and wiped her forehead. 'There. I'm finished.'

'I love this. This is great. This is fabulous,' he said, bursting out laughing and hugging her. 'I didn't realize you had all that anger and pain in you. I really didn't realize you could scream this loud and this honestly. I mean that was great, really *great*.'

'This is not a show, you know,' she answered sternly, pushing him away. 'Is everything a show to you, a game? What do you think this is, entertainment?'

'No, of course not,' he answered gently.

She threw him out of her studio. 'Don't come back,' she said.

He didn't.

She started dreaming about him again. She sat by the telephone waiting for him to call. She hated him.

One week later he called, and before he could say anything she told him to come over. He was there ten minutes later.

He told her he could easily fall in love with her.

Later, when they were lying in bed and he appeared to be sleeping, she whispered in his ear that she had been in love with him all along.

He moved in with her.

One morning, a year later, she woke up earlier than him. She looked at him. A strange feeling came over her. He didn't move her any more. He didn't stir deep emotions in her any more. All that she had loved in him suddenly appeared stale. Used. Like a piece of clothing that had been worn for too long.

He opened his eyes and looked at her. 'What's the matter?' he asked.

'Nothing,' she said.

The Nabi

The Old City is covered with a soft pink and grey light. It is getting close to dusk. Adrian puts his hand around his wife's slender waist and feels the light cotton fabric of her short orange dress.

'Let's go home,' he says. 'Let's go back to the hotel. I'm tired.'

'Oh, come on, let's just take one last walk. You promised.' Miriam tugs at his sleeve and he shakes his head in disbelief.

'I don't know where you get all this energy ... God, Miriam, we've been walking for –' Adrian glances at his watch and counts quickly '– we've been walking for practically four hours and—'

'Let's not exaggerate. We had an hour-long lunch break. That was so nice, that restaurant, and that whole part of Jerusalem is like a dream, with all those cypress trees, Bauhaus and Arab houses ... It's a really nice city, don't you think?'

'Hmmm,' Adrian mumbles.

'I know. You like Greece better, because it's more comfortable, more like paradise, more like a typical honeymoon place.'

'So what's wrong with that? What's wrong with lying on beaches like we did in Greece?'

'Nothing at all. It was great!' Miriam responds cheerfully. 'But,' and here she eyes Adrian scrupulously, 'I do think you have a special little thing for Greece, after the very special little adventure you had with that Teodora girl you were so nuts about—'

'Oh, come on . . . Leave poor Teodora alone. She ended up married to some older guy and produced five children. Not exactly a happy ending is it . . . ?'

'Why not? Maybe she's really happy with her five kids.'

'Maybe. Now. Can we head back? I'm zonked.'

Miriam smiles at him. His face is tanned, his light brown eyes are more puffy than usual. She passes her hand through his curly dark hair. 'I'm having a wonderful honeymoon,' she whispers provocatively in his ear.

'So am I,' he answers back, smiling at her. She wishes he would have whispered back to her, and this thought somehow coincides with the slightly troubling conclusion she has drawn about him, namely that he lacks spontaneity and seems to monitor his curiosity, as if he were afraid of both his and Miriam's mind luring him into unknown territories.

Miriam and Adrian got married recently. They lived together for four months before he proposed to her as they were coming out of a Paris cinema.

Their wedding ceremony was intimate, the reception modest. As they left the party later on that night, Adrian kissed his bride passionately and Miriam thought to herself that she couldn't possibly be happier than this. But since then, several aspects of Adrian's character have become apparent (his systematic need to be in control of everything in his life), tainting the idea she previously had of him, a thought she attributed to her having lived so little time with him and having been blinded by the infatuation she felt for him.

'I'm glad to hear this,' her friend Anne said, when Miriam voiced her concerns. 'It's about time you discovered his imperfections. Until now, he was too perfect to be true. I was getting worried! And I'll tell you something else: I'm sure that Adrian is equally irritated by things you do, things he was unaware of before.'

'Like what?' Miriam exclaimed.

'I don't know,' Anne answered, 'but I'm sure he is!'

As she remembers Anne's words, Miriam feels reassured. Indeed, any of these misgivings are perfectly normal, considering the little amount of time they have known each other. She grabs Adrian's hand and leads the way into a maze of picturesque streets.

After seeing a sign indicating the Arab quarter, she takes a left turn. Adrian follows complacently. As they walk, Miriam notices that the streets have emptied, but decides not to mention it. After about a quarter of a mile Adrian exclaims, 'Miriam! Where are we? Where did everybody go? Let's get out of here, I've got a bad feeling. Let's turn around. Now.'

'Why should we turn around? We're on an adventure,' Miriam argues. 'And honeymoons are not only about relaxing but also about adventures.'

'Not in my book, they're not. Come on Miriam, let's go home, I'm exhausted.'

As she half-heartedly acquiesces, all the while complaining about Adrian's lack of courage, they suddenly find themselves in front of a barricade of Israeli soldiers with automatic rifles slung on their shoulders.

'What are you doing here?' one of the soldiers asks them, blocking their way. 'You cannot come in here. It's forbidden.'

'Why?' Miriam exclaims.

'Why? Because it's closed off. Hasn't anybody told you?' the soldier asks aggressively. 'There's been an attack.'

'What happened?' Miriam enquires anxiously.

'A civilian has been wounded, another one is dead. You cannot come in here.'

'God, I can't believe this,' Adrian mutters. 'Could you tell us which way Jaffa Gate is?'

'Turn right and go straight. You won't miss it. Shalom.'

'I told you,' Adrian hisses, as they retrace their steps away from the barricade, 'I told you we shouldn't be here. Now, will you listen to me next time or what? God, that was so embarrassing, just standing in front of those soldiers and having to admit that I didn't know about an attack which the whole world probably knows about by now. I hate being in this kind of situation.' Adrian kicks a pebble on the ground, and fumbles in his shirt pocket for his pack of cigarettes. 'Shit. And I ran out of cigarettes. Great timing.' His lips purse together in anger as he throws the empty pack on the side of the cobblestone street.

'You shouldn't just throw that thing anywhere,' Miriam remarks, avoiding his gaze.

'It's not just a thing. It's my pack of cigarettes,' he snaps.

'All right. It's your pack of cigarettes. And why are you in such a bad mood anyway?'

'What do you think?' He starts shouting. 'You think it's

fun to pretend to be a moronic tourist? You think that's fun?'

'You didn't have to pretend anything, I did,' Miriam snaps back, raising her voice as well. 'And I wasn't in the least embarrassed about it.'

'You weren't? Well, good for you.'

Adrian puts his hands in his pockets, a solemn expression on his face. 'Miriam,' he finally says, 'I guess what really bothers me is the fact that you never seem to listen to me.'

'I do listen to you.'

'No, you don't. You like to have things your way. You're stubborn.'

'All right, I'm sorry!' she vociferates. 'Next time I'll listen to you!' She throws her hair back and mutters something incomprehensible.

'I'm glad you're sorry, but I'll be even happier when we get the hell out of here. Let's just go back to our hotel. We'll spend the whole evening under the covers, and tomorrow morning we'll order breakfast in bed again.' He puts his arm around Miriam and kisses her cheek.

She remains silent.

'What is it?' Adrian asks her, his arm still around her.

'Nothing. I was just realizing that this is our first fight since we got married.'

'So it is,' Adrian answers, 'although I wouldn't really call it a fight. More like an argument.'

'No, a fight.'

'No, an argument!'

Their voices rise, soon broken by laughter. After a while, the change of neighbourhood is visible. The streets are once again populated with Arabs who are packing up their goods in order to go home. Within a few minutes most vegetable and fruit stands are shut down. The jewellery displays (large, colourful stone necklaces, ivory bracelets, fake lapis lazuli rings) are still attracting customers. There are also shabby looking cafés where groups of men sit talking and smoking, as Arab music pours into the spice-scented street.

As they immerse themselves further into the quaint Jewish quarter, Miriam squeezes Adrian's hand. She feels the sweat of his palm against hers, a sure sign of nervousness.

'What's the matter now?' she asks him, trying to keep her voice from sounding irritated.

'I don't know, I guess I'm just more of a "Club Med" kind of guy . . . The idea of walking on a street where two guys were attacked just moments ago makes me nervous.'

'My God, Adrian, you've got to be joking. I didn't marry a "Club Med" kind of guy, did I?' she asks him, and this time her voice sounds troubled.

'No, I guess I was exaggerating. What I'm trying to say is that we're here on a honeymoon, not to become the next news headlines. Who knows if they arrested the terrorist who stabbed those guys? Who knows anything around here anyway?' He kicks another pebble in front of him and his face takes on a sombre look.

'Nobody knows anything around here, and they're trying to sort that out. All they know is that they want peace. At least some of them do.' Miriam speaks calmly, avoiding Adrian's gaze.

'Well, count me as among those who want peace. And

quiet. And a nice cool bath with a very, very large Scotch and soda brought to me by my beautiful wife. That will be my peace.'

Miriam smiles at him and squeezes his hand. They walk back towards Jaffa Gate where they exit the Old City and follow the main road back towards their hotel.

'My peace will come when we are a family,' Miriam declares. 'I think children are great. When I visit my sister and her husband they seem so happy with their children. When do you think you'll be ready to start a family?'

Adrian looks startled. 'Frankly, I have no idea. Why are we talking about children? What does it have to do with anything else?'

'Well, it does have something to do with peace doesn't it? Look at this country: if Israelis and Palestinians started having children together, it could bring peace to this part of the world. Children have something to do with everything, don't they? I don't know, I guess this is as good a time to bring it up as any.'

'We've brought it up several times. I told you, I'm not ready to have children just yet,' Adrian replies, annoyed. 'Can we switch topics?'

'Well, frankly, I prefer talking about our future together, as opposed to how nervous you're feeling. It's boring. So tell me. If you don't see us having children right away, when do you think will be a good time?'

'First of all, we just got married, Miriam. I'd like to enjoy being married for a while, before becoming a father. Second of all, well, I thought that with your acting career and everything you'd prefer to wait ... But I guess I was wrong.' His voice dims a little.

'What's the matter, my love?' she asks him softly. 'You don't want children right away? Well, that's fine. We can wait. You're probably right. I should concentrate on my acting career for now.'

'You should. You've got everything it takes to be a star. I've always told you that. Anyway –' he puts his arm around her – 'let's just play it by ear. We'll have children whenever the time seems appropriate.'

'I don't believe in an appropriate time to get pregnant,' she answers firmly.

'Well, there is.' He smiles.

'I don't think so,' she disagrees.

'Now. Will you walk a little faster, or do you want to have a discussion here until dark and we're really done for?'

'I love it when you overreact,' she says, putting her two hands around his waist and kissing his neck.

Adrian sighs and looks at her. Her body looks tanned and slim, her blue eyes are sparkling in the early evening light, her light brown hair is laden with golden streaks and as she laughs he feels his heart sink.

'I love you,' he says to her. 'I'm madly in love with you.'

'That's why you married me!' She smiles as she presses her warm lips against his. He softly leans her head against the large white stones, and runs his long fingers along her curvaceous body, stopping to caress her firm breasts. As he presses himself delightfully against her he feels her arms caressing his back, sliding down to his waist. This causes him to lose his self-control. He suddenly stops, realizing that in this particular place their actions might provoke condemnation. He immediately regains his composure and orders her to follow him quickly.

As she shrugs her shoulders and arranges her dress, an Arab man comes out of one of the small stone houses that line the street and mutters something to them.

'Let's go,' Adrian immediately snaps, 'let's go right now.'

'Relax,' Miriam retorts, 'you're really starting to drive me crazy.'

'I just want to get back to that damn hotel of ours.'

'We're going, what else do you think we're doing?'

As they are making their way out of the Old City, Miriam suddenly notices a striking-looking man. He is sitting on a small stool in the middle of a courtyard. She motions Adrian to stop. As she ventures closer, she notices that he is holding a glass of mint tea in one hand and large playing cards are lying on a table in front of him.

'Look, Adrian, look!' she exclaims.

'Now what.' He sighs.

'I want to talk to this amazing-looking man,' she says in a decided tone of voice, which by now, Adrian knows better than to argue against.

'Fine.' He surrenders, noticing a small bench where a frail old Arab woman sits, wearing a torn colourful dress, her head covered by a blue scarf. She is skinning luscious red watermelons, removing their seeds and dropping them into a bowl full of water. 'I'll sit next to this woman,' he announces in a small voice, as if he has just lost some kind of battle, 'and when you're through investigating this very unusual man, come and get me. You can't miss me. I'll be sitting right here, probably helping out with the water-melons.'

She laughs and kisses him tenderly. 'I love you so much,' she whispers to him, 'I really do.'

He tries to appear oblivious to her comment, sitting down next to the old woman on what appears to be a fairly unstable bench, but as Miriam walks away he calls her back. 'I love you,' he says, reaching out towards her. As she comes near to him he holds her against him and runs his fingers around her silky skin. 'Don't take too long,' he says almost shyly, and as she's about to answer the old woman looks at them and smiles; she has no teeth.

'He a Nabi,' she tells them, pointing towards the man on the stool.

'A what?' they ask in unison.

'A Nabi,' she repeats, 'a prophet.'

'He's a prophet?' Miriam enquires in an excited voice.

'Yes,' the old woman answers. 'He tells future. Very well. He very famous.'

'I told you!' Miriam exclaims. 'I told you that man looked amazing! Okay, I'll be right back.' She dashes off, before Adrian can say anything.

Her legs tremble in anticipation as she approaches the Nabi. She's always dreamed of seeing a fortune-teller, ever since she was small. But her desire has always been tainted with fear. Now she feels stronger, ready to expect almost anything. Being married makes her feel more self-confident, more adventurous. And she likes proving her strength to Adrian.

She approaches the Nabi timidly. Although he is sitting

down, it is quite obvious that he is very tall. His long legs are stretched out and his pants are too short. They show off thin ankles and dirty, broken toenails that stick out from under his ragged sandals. His dark skin is inhabited by wrinkles. His hair is practically gone, but his blue eyes bear a youthful buoyancy that makes Miriam uncertain about his age.

He looks at her carefully and points towards another stool that stands underneath an orange tree in the back of the courtyard. As she goes to get it she looks at Adrian, who seems immersed in a conversation with the old woman. She waves but not daring to call out his name, quickly gives up when she realizes he isn't looking up.

'You can sit here,' the Nabi says in English, in a low and deep voice.

'Thank you,' she answers, blushing for no reason.

He asks her to put five cards face down. She complies with utmost concentration. He lowers his wrinkled face towards the cards (Miriam wonders if it's because of poor eyesight), then lifts them up with excruciating care, as if they were made of thin sheets of crystal.

As he turns each one of them around in the air, it is as if he is making the cards float, moving his bony hand steadily downward, like the soft wings of a bird. Then, as his hand seemingly wavers, planning its landing, he closes his eyes. He only opens them when the cards are impeccably fanned on the table, right side up.

He looks at them a long time before talking. Miriam thinks she notices a frown on his face as he observes the cards. She is about to get impatient when he starts talking.

Slowly, steadily, in fairly good English. He doesn't look up at her.

'You are just married,' he starts. 'Your husband works with money. His mother is unhappy, you fight with her too much. She is a good woman. Your family is different. I see love everywhere in your family. A lot of love. Almost too much. You have two brothers and one of them is not well.'

He pauses and she can hear his breathing. She feels a swelling in her throat because in this short time the Nabi has only spoken the truth. Adrian is a banker, his mother is a good woman and she has been a bit hard on her. Her parents have had a happy marriage and her younger brother has been experiencing complications resulting from the removal of his appendix.

Miriam suddenly shivers. She is afraid to hear any more. She turns around and looks at Adrian again. This time he sees her and waves at her, his arms move to and fro, reminding her of the arms of a windmill.

She turns back towards the Nabi, almost painfully, not wanting to let go of Adrian's gaze. She thinks about getting up and telling the Nabi she's heard enough. After all, she has the right to do so, she's paying him. As she is about to announce her departure the Nabi starts talking again. She feels trapped. She must stay and listen. Suddenly, she feels as if her life depends on it.

'You are working on –' here he hesitates '– You are working for the cinema. Yes. People will know your face. It will one day be very famous. (Here a smile escapes Miriam; that was too easy, she says to herself. But as for the cinema bit, well, once again he has surprised her.)

'Your face will be famous (she almost detects a smile and wonders if he's making fun of her). And many men will want you. And you will choose another man.'

'What?' she exclaims. 'Why should I? I love my husband!'

'Yes, you do. But your husband cannot have children.'

'What?' she whispers this time.

'Your husband knows but is afraid to tell you. He will not tell you until it is too late. He cannot have children.'

Miriam feels as if she has just been slapped by an invisible hand. It cannot be true. Adrian would have told her. But then again, would he? And after all, who says this fortune-teller knows what he's talking about? Yes, really, why should she trust this man?

The Nabi's voice has suddenly got lower. 'You must decide if you will tell him you know. He will not admit to you, but you will know it is the truth. Your husband will never be able to have children. You can pay me in dollars. Five dollars. And please put the chair back under the tree. Thank you, Madame, and goodbye.'

She gets up slowly and feels the blood rush to her head. She fumbles for her money and hands him a five-dollar bill. She places the chair back under the tree. She looks towards the small bench. Adrian isn't sitting there any more, neither is the old woman. She looks around, her knees weakening, then staggers over to the small bench and sits down. Her foot almost knocks over the bowl of water that stands on the ground. She looks down. There is a pile of watermelon rinds on the ground and she picks one of them up. It is wet and soothing and she applies it to her burning cheeks. Her mouth feels very dry. She swallows hard and decides that she will not let the Nabi's words get to her. But somewhere, in the bottom of her swelling heart, she feels they might be true.

She gets up again and slowly walks around the courtyard. She calls out Adrian's name. There is no answer. She sees the Nabi stacking his cards together and taking another sip of his mint tea.

Her voice is now trembling as she cries out for Adrian. She is about to leave the courtyard when she suddenly sees him emerging from one of the white stone houses opposite, holding what looks like a bag of green grapes in his hand and waving goodbye to the old woman he was sitting next to. As Miriam calls out his name again, he waves to her cheerfully and motions her to wait for him on that same bench.

As she walks back towards it, she sees him go up to the Nabi and watches him go through the same motions as she did, getting the little stool from under the orange tree.

She approaches the bench, then sits down and starts crying silently. She watches Adrian's back as he listens to the Nabi. She watches as part of the sky now turns a darker blue, while further on the horizon it is still a glorious pink.

She waits for Adrian to turn around and look at her. He doesn't. She watches him bend his head towards the Nabi and scratch the back of his neck.

She sees the old woman coming out of her little house again. Upon seeing her she stops crying, and watches as she walks unbearably slowly. As she approaches the small bench, Miriam notices she has brought a plastic bag with her.

The old woman starts taking the seeds out of the bowl

and puts a handful of them in the plastic bag. Her back is bent in pain and her gentle eyes plead for Miriam to help her in her endeavour.

As she bends down again and again, the old woman's mouth contorts itself in an ugly grimace. Miriam remains impassive, unable to move. She tries to reach her hand out towards the old woman, but stops in mid-air and lets it drop heavily on her lap. The old woman looks at her again, and this time her eyes have stopped pleading.

Miriam watches her move her old hands to and from the bag. She sits until Adrian calls her, and by that time it is dark and they head back towards their hotel in silence.

Discordance

Sandra decided to leave Jeremy. Not because of the fact that he still lived with his girlfriend, but because she wasn't in love with him. Ever since Nathan, her last boyfriend, she felt as if she had been drained of any emotion whatsoever, of the energy and desire which is prevalent when falling in love. She compared herself to a stream that suddenly ran dry. Not to say that she wasn't attracted to Jeremy. On the contrary. Every time she saw him, she found herself more attracted to him. The attraction was a slow and gradual process, which had begun as mere curiosity on her part when on that first evening they spent together, at a crowded and smoky party, he surprised her by motioning her to follow him into a room and wrapped his arms around her. As he leaned her gently against the wall, the sound of an electric guitar infiltrated her body and his warm lips touched hers, almost too eagerly and somewhat clumsily. She reciprocated his kiss, her eyes half-open, her hands tightly pressed together behind her back.

He felt her uneasiness, she thought, but chose not to say anything about it until much later on, when the first signs of dawn started to surface through the Manhattan sky and they left the party. Their blending together was inevitable, he tried to explain to her. She objected to his use of the word 'blending'. It conveyed intimate images of a unison, an evocation which she deemed far too precocious on his part. Sandra had always been opposed to the categorization of moments, however special they might be. And this one was far from anything special; it was an event which, at least for now, did not bear any particular significance to her other than that she had let herself be seduced by a man for whom she had tepid feelings.

She didn't share these thoughts with him but listened to Jeremy as he went on talking. Even though he was still very attached to his girlfriend, he continued (he carefully avoided the word love), he felt himself being so drawn to Sandra, that at this point nothing could stop him.

Sandra remarked that this might lead to a difficult situation. She told him about Nathan, about the fact that she had lived through a tumultuous and painful experience with him, and that she was still recovering from him. Then she paused for an instant, reflecting on this verb she had just attributed to a man she had loved so much, a man she had been willing to marry, even though they had only been together for six months. Indeed, she was recovering from Nathan as if he had been a disease she had been afflicted with, a disease whose scars she still felt healing slowly within her.

Jeremy didn't reply, perhaps out of deference, or merely out of sheer disinterest. She didn't pursue the topic and agreed to have a last cup of coffee with him before he headed back home.

They sat down in a dismal coffee shop, where the only other clients were an elderly drunken man, who kept mumbling incomprehensible words to himself, and a tired-looking Hispanic waiter with a large tattoo of a spider on his forearm.

She asked him questions about Alice, his girlfriend. She wondered about her. She recalled the night she had met both Jeremy and Alice. It was at a surprise party Laura had organized for her boyfriend Leo. They had all been sitting around drinking white wine and eating crisps when the doorbell rang and more guests poured in. Sandra had met Jeremy before, at his small gallery in SoHo. She had been to one of his openings, a crowded and fashionable event, and remembered being intrigued by him. Now she saw him in a different setting, holding his girlfriend by the hand, a stunning-looking woman in her early twenties, with high cheekbones, deep soft eyes and luminescent skin.

The fact that she was so beautiful made Jeremy all the more appealing to Sandra. She had an urge to find out more about him, to talk to him. He was in his early thirties, of medium height, with a receding hairline and dark inquisitive eyes. If taken apart, his features were not especially striking. But as a whole there was something quite charming about him, quite appealing actually. Despite his serious expression, Sandra noticed a sparkle in his eyes that seemed to betray a vague cynicism of sorts, or sapient intuition, that led her to feel inexplicably drawn to him. As she was talking to him, Alice walked over and smiled at both of them. Sandra immediately froze, gave her full attention to Alice and decided that this was certainly not worth the trouble. And not only that, but she didn't feel intrigued enough by him to pursue anything. Least of all breaking up their relationship.

She found herself thinking about him the next day, but in a distant and almost friendly way. Maybe she could go out one evening with both of them, she said to herself.

Jeremy called her the following day, and mentioned something about a party an art-critic friend they had in common was throwing that night. Sandra agreed to meet him at a bar on Prince Street at ten o'clock, and was surprised to find him standing alone in the cold, his hands buried in the pockets of a long white raincoat. She asked him where Alice was. She doesn't like art-people parties, he grinned. She dropped the topic and followed him to a giant loft where a large number of people in ragged clothes were spread out, drinking beer out of plastic glasses and smoking cigarettes.

'Almost everyone here is broke,' Jeremy remarked.

It was later on that night that he kissed her. Several days later, they made love. She found no pleasure in the act, performing the usual gestures mechanically, indifferently. She even found herself thinking about something else, something which had absolutely nothing to do with the fact that a man was lying in her arms, seemingly taking great pleasure in the act, as demonstrated by his rapid panting and final loud cry of victory, marking the end of the shortest session of lovemaking she had ever gone through.

When he got up and said he needed to take a shower before he went home for reasons that she could probably guess, Sandra wondered what it was exactly that had led her to accept the role of being 'the other woman'. As she looked at her clock she noticed that they had spent exactly ten minutes in bed and she decided that there were two reasons why she was allowing herself to go through with this. One was because she didn't want to be alone. The other was because she felt less vulnerable as the lover than she did as the girlfriend: as the lover she had nothing to lose. The fact that a barrier had already been imposed between them made it astonishingly easy to bear; this was a dead end. She wasn't curious about what lay beyond the warning signs, and she didn't ever expect to find out. But as the girlfriend she had all to lose, as had been demonstrated by her behaviour in her last three relationships: gradual infatuation, mounting subserviency and inevitable disappointment.

Sandra resented her own weakness and the fact that ever since Michael, with whom she had lived for two years in perfect harmony and boredom, she had lost touch with what her mother called 'appropriate behaviour'. How long would it take before she fell for yet another man? And when would she finally be able to spend more than three months alone?

Such was the depressing status of her current love life. It couldn't go on like this; there was no doubt about it. She needed to find her own epicentre, gain a perspective that would render her actions justifiable; for now, she saw them merely as impulsive.

She noticed how wide a gap there was between her personal and professional life. Her career as a concert pianist was slowly starting to take off (she was giving her second solo recital that month) and yet it wasn't enough to satisfy her. She was spoiled; she needed everything. Full attention, constant drama. She had to stop being attracted to men who were passionate about her in a self-destructive way, and she had to break the habit of reciprocating their passion, a compassionate gesture which often turned against her. It was time for her to prove to herself that she could be on her own. She didn't like Jeremy enough to want to give a part of herself up for him. Actually, when she thought about it seriously, she could find no reason for being with him, except that he seemed to be quite enamoured of her, a symptom which at this point was losing its appeal.

So as she watched him towel himself dry after his shower, adding mountains of deodorant to his underarms ('Won't that make Alice even more suspicious?' she couldn't help herself asking, to which he didn't respond but made an unattractive face in the mirror), she decided to tell him that it would probably be best for both of them if they made this their last meeting together. She was about to start talking when the phone rang. It was her friend Sofia from Athens, telling her she had great news. Sandra, eager to speak to her friend, whispered to Jeremy that she had to take this call, why didn't they talk tomorrow. He nodded, looking somewhat annoyed, tied the laces of his shoes with unbearable slowness (anal retentive, Sandra thought to herself, eager to see him leave), and finally, his hair perfectly combed back and his white shirt remarkably uncreased, he waved at her, an almost shy wave, and left rapidly, careful not to slam the front door.

As Sofia told her she was four months pregnant, Sandra felt tears mounting in her eyes. 'Will this ever happen to me?' she wondered, ashamed at her jealous reaction and realizing how much she longed to change her life.

That night she watched television for five hours straight and stayed up until dawn rehearsing her farewell speech to Jeremy.

The next morning she practised a Schubert sonata until noon, when Jeremy called. It was perfect timing; the disparity between the purity of the nineteenth-century music and the sound of his raucous, twentieth-century, insistently blasé voice.

The perfect time to break it off and mean it.

So she did.

But she hadn't been prepared for Jeremy's reaction. As soon as she poured out the line she had rehearsed so well the night before (something about not being ready for a relationship, not being ready to commit to anyone), he immediately started arguing that what they had between them wasn't exactly a relationship, considering the fact that he lived with someone, all it was was a very pleasant diversion.

A diversion.

She repeated the words slowly, not quite knowing how to respond to this surprising definition of what she, in her arrogant mind, had perceived as a growing relationship with a man who seemed to be falling for her.

Her initial reaction of surprise turned to humiliation. 'A diversion from what?' she asked coldly.

'From the current boredom of my life,' he answered simply, as if there was nothing wrong with using her as some kind of object with which he could release his frustrations.

'I see,' Sandra said, so taken aback that for a while she found herself unable to say anything, letting the mouthpiece of the phone dangle somewhere between her left hand and the table it stood on, a tempting though cowardly solution to putting an end to her frustrations.

'Hello?' she heard his voice call out from somewhere in mid-air.

'Yes, I'm here,' she said, grabbing the phone and reluctantly placing it against her ear.

'You're not saying anything, are you upset?' he asked in a way that sounded too familiar, conjuring up images of her past tormented love life, where words of separation were starting to sound eerily similar. How come each parting situation had such limited vocabulary?

'I'm not upset,' she decided to answer, 'I'm just surprised that you're living with someone who you find boring.'

'I never said I find her boring,' he replied defensively.

'Well, what is it then?' Sandra asked, feeling that the conversation had taken on a new turn.

'I don't know,' he answered vaguely, 'maybe it's just myself I'm bored with.'

'Oh.' She felt at once relieved and amused by his words. She was almost tempted to tell him that he was right to feel that way, because she had suddenly come to realize that this was the reason why she didn't want to stay with him. He was, indeed, boring. It was as simple as that. His conversation and insights about life, which she had at first believed to be sagacious and profound, had turned out to be banal and rather insipid. And considering that he had owned a gallery for practically five years, his outlook on the art world had seemed to her surprisingly ignorant of anything that was happening beyond the Atlantic Ocean. 'I don't care too much for foreign artists,' he had told her once. 'There are too many in our own country for us to worry about the foreign ones. I mean New York is the centre of the art world after all, you can't deny that.'

'Sure, but what about the foreign artists who live here?' she had asked him, astounded by how small-minded he sounded.

'Well, some of them are good,' he had ventured.

The click of her call-waiting signal interrupted her thoughts. 'I've got to go,' she said abruptly, 'I've got another call coming in and I have an appointment in a half-hour.'

'Wait!' he said, his voice interrupted by the second click. 'Don't just hang up on me! When am I going to see you again?'

'I don't know, I've got to go,' she said, longing to put an end to this conversation. 'Please, let me hang up.'

He hung up before she did. When she returned to her other line, it was dead, the person had given up. Furious, she slammed down the phone, grabbed her coat and handbag, ran down the stairs of her apartment building and into the subway. She didn't know exactly where she was going; all she knew was that she needed to get out of her apartment and clear up her confused thoughts. She got off the train at 72nd Street and walked towards Central Park. A homeless man asked her for some change, and when she told him she didn't have any, he told her she was lying. Sandra looked at the man disconcerted. 'I'm not lying, and you don't have be so rude,' she reproached him.

'Who gives a fuck if I'm rude?' the homeless man snapped. 'Nobody gives a fuck.'

She shrugged her shoulders and walked away. The man

continued to say 'nobody gives a fuck' until it became a loud scream which she could hear all the way from the bench a few blocks away, where she had seated herself next to a nanny and an infant.

The homeless man's words pierced her heart in an unexpected way, and by the time she had got up and walked back towards Central Park West, her eyes were filled with tears, and she knew that this was the time to forget and move on.

Sandra gave her recital on a winter's day. The public arrived in snow boots, their feet wet from the slush outside, their faces wrapped in heavy woollen scarves, their noses red from the cold. They took a long time to sit down, fussing about in hushed voices. The recital hall was cold and damp, and she worried that her icy fingers would keep her from playing well. But once the coughs and throat clearings subsided and she placed her fingers on the keyboard, a sudden warmth (which she attributed to an adrenalin rush) invaded her fingers, and she began Beethoven's opus 110 with the melodious aplomb the first movement required. Midway through the second movement, a sudden uncontrollable shudder overtook her by surprise and she simultaneously hit an A and a B flat. She felt like stopping right then and there, out of shame and embarrassment, but she knew she couldn't do such a drastic thing. It would ruin all the efforts her agent, Marcy Tannen, had undertaken on her behalf. She caught Marcy's eye as she hit those two chords, but the gaze remained steady. Maybe it wasn't so bad after all.

She was able to find the inspiration she needed for the

third movement, and as she was playing she closed her eyes and let the music pour out of her fingers on to the keyboard which, despite the dampness of the auditorium, retained a beautiful sound. She hit the last chord with a note of relief.

The applause was energetic and spontaneous, and she attacked Schubert's sonata in C minor with a smile on her lips. She pictured herself being flown away with the music, landing on the top of a cliff, surrounded by emptiness. The keyboard was smooth, her fingers glided around it effortlessly. The music was sweet and melancholic at the same time, then suddenly it became more dramatic. She pictured Schubert on his deathbed, his body riddled by syphilis, the looming imminence of his death, the mourning of his admirers, and suddenly it was the end of the piece, she got up to take a bow and the auditorium broke into a feverish clapping which only waned once she had made three repeated encores.

To her surprise, there was a crowd waiting for her backstage. People she had never seen before smiled at her timidly and asked for her autograph. She signed them carefully, suddenly feeling important. Marcy Tannen, Tom Duccio her manager, and the director of the concert hall were making a fuss about her, and she overheard Tom speaking with a tall man about the possibility of signing her up with an established record label.

As she was talking to her parents (they both bore a fixed, proud smile on their lips), she saw Jeremy standing sheepishly in a corner, a small bouquet of roses in his hands. She hadn't expected to see him there, and his presence unnerved her more than anything else.

'That was really nice,' he said to her, handing her the flowers, a faint colour mounting in his cheeks. 'I didn't know you played so well.'

'How did you find out about this concert?' she asked him, consciously trying to keep her voice from sounding irritated.

'You told me about it. Don't you remember?' He looked surprised by her question. 'Are those your parents?' he asked her, switching the conversation to what he presumably thought would be an easier subject to tackle.

'And who is this young man?' Sandra's mother asked, as if she had overheard the whole conversation. She focused her curious eyes on Jeremy's bittersweet smile.

'Mum, Dad,' Sandra said reluctantly, 'this is Jeremy Andrews, a friend.'

'Very nice to meet you,' said Sandra's father, a stout man with a kind face and a German accent.

'Very pleased,' Sandra's mother ventured in a more passive tone.

Both her parents were eager for their eldest daughter to get married (the younger one lived in Connecticut with her husband and two children), and they had of late taken up the bad habit of greeting each male newcomer with a piquant interest they often had trouble disguising, which always caused Sandra undue embarrassment. This evening, though, Sandra was relieved to see her mother acting coolly towards Jeremy, a possible sign that his presence did not imbue in her any kind of expectation, a reaction which Sandra couldn't help but see as an encouraging confirmation of her own tepid feelings towards Jeremy. There was now no doubt in her mind that she didn't want to be with him, and as he asked her what her plans were for the evening, she remained vague, saying that she was probably going out with her parents and her manager.

'Oh,' he said, 'I understand. Well, I guess I'll be seeing you.' He bent over and kissed her cheek.

'Thanks for coming,' she remembered to say.

'You were great,' he told her in all earnestness. 'You really were.'

She couldn't help but feel flattered by the seeming sincerity of his comment. 'Thank you.' She smiled, waving to him as he left.

'Well,' Tom Duccio said, coming towards her, rubbing his hands in a self-congratulatory way, 'we did good tonight. We did real good. You did a good job, Sandra. Keep it up. And I mean that. You're gonna be a star if you go on this way.'

'Who needs to be a star?' Sandra's father remarked. 'As long as she's serious about what she does and she does it well, that's enough for me. What is this star business . . .?'

'Yeah, well I like the star business,' Tom muttered as he motioned a whole group of people, a few of whom Sandra didn't know, to follow him outside.

A table for twelve was waiting for them in a loud midtown Italian trattoria. All the guests raised their glasses and proposed a toast to Sandra. The director of the concert hall said he was going to talk to a few of his other friends in the music industry. Tom Duccio stood up and announced that a star was born. Marcy Tannen whispered to Sandra, 'We're proud of you,' while the latter's mother smiled at her daughter with tears in her eyes.

All these expectations were suddenly bestowed upon

Sandra, and although there was something exhilarating about having her talent publicly confirmed, there was something frightening about it as well. Sandra had never enjoyed having the spotlight on her. She preferred to hide in a corner rather than have people expect anything from her. Whether this was due to shyness or laziness, was something that she hadn't yet figured out. All she knew was that it was easier to hide, and only seldom had it ever made her feel that she was wasting her talent. But that evening, as she was sharing the antipasto with everyone else, she understood that she now had to put those days behind her. She could no longer hide; she had to be visible to those who expected her to be, and, more frightening than anything else, she could no longer afford to deceive anyone. She had to rise higher and make it seem as if it was the easiest thing in the world to do.

She got home late that night, her cheeks covered with kisses and perfume smells, her hands full of blossoming flowers, her ears resonating with the sound of congratulatory words and expectations, and her heart burdened by the fear of disappointing the world.

Jeremy called every day after the concert. He sent Sandra flowers and left sugary messages on her answering machine, each time disregarding the fact that she never called him back. One rainy evening, as she was practising Chopin's ballade number 1, in preparation for an upcoming concert in St Louis, Missouri, the buzzer downstairs rang. It was Jeremy, asking to come upstairs. 'Why?' she asked, annoyed by the interruption. 'I'm working,' she added in a voice too low for him to hear. 'I need to talk to you!' she heard him shout into the buzzer, his other words drowned out by the sound of rain and static.

She let him in. She looked at herself in the mirror and let her hair down. She pulled on the skirt she was wearing so that it looked longer than it actually was. She ran into the bathroom to brush her teeth and managed to straighten out the living-room sofa before he rang the doorbell. When she answered the door she was out of breath and even more annoyed with herself – with the fact that she had felt the need to perform all these aesthetic tasks, all this for a man whom she didn't care about in the least.

'Hi there,' Jeremy said, standing in the doorway, wearing a drenched raincoat. 'I was just passing through your neighbourhood. I got out of work early and thought it would be a good idea to just drop by and talk. I've been trying to get in touch with you for a while.' He asked where he should put his wet umbrella (she told him to put it in the bathtub), took off his raincoat and kissed her on both cheeks. He was wearing an elegant grey suit with a loud red and blue striped tie. He seemed more vulnerable than the other times she had seen him, almost intimidated by her presence, a fact that only served to irritate her more; what was he doing here, standing like a nervous schoolboy? She had been grappling through the Chopin ballade, it was thoroughly challenging, she was wondering if she was ever going to break through the piece, muster its darkest moments, master its complex melody and impossibly rapid crescendo.

'I'm sorry to show up like this,' Jeremy's voice came floating in her ear. 'I just, you know, wanted to talk to you and you haven't been returning my calls.'

She was going to exploit his vulnerability, she said to herself right then and there. She was going to make him feel small and weak and stupid. She was going to humiliate him and show him how pathetic he was.

'What do you want to talk about?' she asked him coldly.

'I wanted to talk about you and me. May I?' He pointed to the sofa and sat down before she could say anything.

'I was working,' she said to him in an equally cold voice. 'I've got a lot of practising to do, so make it quick.'

'I know you're probably mad at me,' he started saying, 'and I can understand that.'

'Why would I be mad?' she asked, genuinely surprised by his comment, and wondering why indeed she was supposed to be mad at him. The fleeting moments they had spent together seemed to be a distant memory which bore no relevance to her current life.

'You're mad because I treated you like the other woman kind of thing, and it really was pretty shitty of me. I'd like to make it up to you and start all over again. I'm on the verge of breaking up with Alice, things have been really rough between us. I'd like you to give me a second chance. I really like you, and when I heard you play the other night, there was this unbelievable intensity about you, an intensity which really spoke to me. I want us to try it out again.'

Sandra was taken aback by his proposition. 'What makes you think I'm interested in getting back together with you?' she asked him in a gentler tone than she intended.

'I don't think it, I'm just hoping it,' he answered candidly.

This was starting to be amusing, Sandra thought, and not entirely unpleasant.

'Unfortunately, Jeremy, your hopes don't have a place in my heart any longer,' she answered, although immediately afterwards she wondered why she had uttered such a lyrical sentence when all she wanted to express was a basic and pragmatic fact.

'You don't know me well at all. There are sides to me you'd be surprised to discover.'

'Oh, yeah? Like what?' she asked him sarcastically, wondering what he was getting at.

'Dark sides,' Jeremy answered, adjusting his tie in the process.

'Let me guess. You like to tie Alice up to your bedpost, blindfold and whip her.'

'No, not quite,' he answered, obviously disturbed by her hypothesis.

'So, what then?' Her curiosity kept her from asking him to leave right then and there, and she suddenly felt oddly threatened by his presence.

'Just dark things in general. I can't exactly start to explain them. It's just that I think that we have more things in common than you realize. Do you have anything to drink?'

'Maybe. By the way, is this what you came to tell me? That you have a dark side I don't know about and that I should explore it?' The threat of his presence quickly give way to resentment. 'What makes you think I'd be interested? What makes you think I even care? I don't know you, that you're right about, and I don't feel the urge to know you. Not in the least. Now, if you don't mind, I've got to get back to my piano.'

'You're obviously still upset with me—'

'I'm not upset, goddammit!' she shouted. 'I just want you to get out of here!'

He got up and walked towards her with a strange, angry expression on his face. As he got closer she noticed that his eyes seemed to be steaming with desire, his pupils were darker and fiercer, his cheeks redder and his overall expression daunting, as if he had suddenly turned into an older man.

He grabbed Sandra's arms and pressed her against the kitchen wall with such force that she couldn't respond in any way. He wrapped his body around hers and started kissing her in a forceful way, ripping her clothes off with unusual dexterity. 'I want you to play the piano naked for me,' he whispered to her.

His unexpected demand sent an eerie chill through her body. She wanted to laugh at him, tell him this was just too ridiculous, but she found herself unable to. Instead, she followed his orders like an automaton. All her previous feelings of inner strength had now given way to a sexual submission that she decided to explore.

She sat down, stark naked, and started to play the Chopin ballade. She heard Jeremy pouring himself a drink. The rain outside was getting thicker, it banged against her window pane with loud insistence, her fingers ran smoothly across the keyboard, and it was not until she was halfway through the piece that she realized she was playing it almost flawlessly, overcoming all the previous difficulties she had experienced. This served to heighten her sexual desire for Jeremy. She played passionately, pouring all her jumbled thoughts on to the keyboard with unmitigated delight. For the first time in a long while, she came to recognize what she had always opposed: this was undeniably a special moment, and one she would have enjoyed even more with the right person. Did this mean that she had become too cynical over the years? That it was time to face her own vulnerability?

She had barely finished the piece when Jeremy was all over her, kissing her body amorously, his breath full of whisky and the taste of her lip gloss. He had his shirt and tie still on, but his pants were off. He asked her to lie down on the piano bench and penetrated her right there and then. It was exciting and pathetic at the same time, she thought, because he was so obviously trying to prove something to her.

Despite these cogitations she yielded to him, because this time his body felt warm and pleasant and strong, although she once again failed to achieve any kind of pleasure with him, because, as she now understood, there was a discordance between their bodies and souls. They would never be able to carry a perfectly synchronous melody together.

This thought coincided with the end of their love-making session, at which point Jeremy gave her a quick kiss on the stomach, got up, took a sip of his whisky and went back to sitting on the sofa, a bemused grin on his face.

Sandra collected her clothes and closed her bedroom door as she quickly put them back on, disgusted with herself and the fact that she had given in to him once again. When she returned to the living room, he was still sitting there, although his clothes were now back on as well, and he bore a more serious look on his face.

'Jeremy,' she said in a tired voice, 'this shouldn't have happened. I don't know why I let it happen, but one thing I know is this: you have to leave now. You really do.'

'You want me to leave? Now?' He seemed both shocked and offended.

'Yes. I do.'

'And what if I tell you that I don't want to leave?'

'It's my house. I don't care what you want. I know what I want.' She uttered these harsh words with surprising composure.

'Fine. You want me to leave, I'll leave. But don't expect to see me again.'

'I'm not expecting anything.'

He looked at her disdainfully. 'I don't get you. I really don't.'

'I'm not asking you to "get me", Jeremy.' She felt compelled to give him an explanation of sorts. 'It's just that I'm wondering why I did what I just did, and I need to be alone to think about it.'

'It's funny,' he said in a strained voice, 'I was always under the impression that women hated men who took off right after screwing them. I guess I was wrong.'

'Just go,' she mumbled in a hushed voice.

'Sure, I'll go,' Jeremy answered, 'since you really know what you want, don't you? Everything is so clear in that little mind of yours, isn't it?'

'Yes, it is,' she answered, hurt by his definition of her mind. 'It is clear. I want you to leave.'

'Fine. It was nice seeing you again. Good luck with your piano playing.'

He put on his raincoat. As he walked towards the front door and opened it, letting cold air into the apartment, she suddenly felt a strong combination of yearning and disappointment, like a little girl who knows she wants something but cannot find the proper words to express exactly what it is she wants. 'Fuck you, Jeremy,' she said, out of the blue.

'Why are you saying that?' he asked her, clearly taken aback by her statement.

'I don't know,' she whispered.

Jeremy closed the front door and she heard his heavy footsteps going down the stairs. She finished the whisky he had left on the kitchen table. It burnt her cheeks, and she felt the urge to splash some cold water on her face. She walked towards the bathroom. Suddenly, she froze: there, in her rusty bathtub, lay his umbrella, its black flaps sprawled open like a sick bird.

The Wedding

That morning, the maid came in twenty minutes late. When Mme Bresson asked her how come she was so late, that wasn't customary of her, and how come she smelled of smoke, in the five years she had worked for her she had never known her to smoke, the maid answered placidly that she was really sorry, but something unusual had happened that morning. Then she paused a little until Mme Bresson asked her what this unusual thing was, and the maid told her that Pablo, her boyfriend, had asked to marry her. He had asked her at seven thirty that morning, and they had talked about it until eight thirty. That was why she was so late, since, as Mme Bresson might already know, it takes her almost an hour to get to her house every morning, just getting to the Métro was a long walk and—

Mme Bresson interrupted her and told her there really wasn't much time to talk right now, there was a lot of work to do, but she was very happy for her and wished her all the happiness in the world. Then she asked her how long she had known her friend and Maria answered one year. Mme Bresson told her that one year was time enough to get to know someone very well, and it gave one ample time to think about future plans thoroughly. Maria said yes, Mme Bresson, and followed her into the kitchen where she was shown the shopping list for that morning. Then Maria changed into her white uniform and started sweeping the floor. She was a short brunette, with large expressive eyes and pale lips. She was slightly overweight, with small plump legs. She never wore make-up and her hair was always neatly combed into a bun. She couldn't have been more than twenty-five years old, though her face bore the scars of an enduring life.

Maria once told Emma, Mme Bresson's daughter, about her life. She came from the suburbs of Cascais, Portugal, from a family of nine children. Her father was a farmer, her mother didn't work since she had spent the first fourteen years with her husband being pregnant (though after all the children were born she helped around the Vasconsuelos bakery in the next town). When she was sixteen Maria had to stop school because her parents needed her around the house. When she was seventeen, they put great pressure on her to marry M. Vasconsuelos' son, Fernando, but she couldn't do it. Though he was much better off than most of the families in her town, she couldn't picture herself living with someone like him for the rest of her life. He was ugly and loud, and the only time he invited her for a drink he made her pay for it. So her parents gave up, and her sister Isabella married him instead. But whether she was happy or not, Maria told Emma, she wasn't quite sure, since they moved to the Algarve, where he opened his own bakery, and they seldom visited each other. All she knew about her was that when she did see Isabella, she felt as if she had lost a sister.

At the age of twenty, Maria moved to Paris. She learned French quickly and was lucky enough to find a job almost right away. At first, she worked for a rich family who lived in a large house with a garden, but they moved to America.

So she started working for the Bressons and they treated her well. Emma told her she was happy to hear that because they liked her. The conversation was left at that because Mme Bresson called Emma in and told her to let Maria work in peace. She asked her to go and finish her studying instead because, at this pace, she'd never pass her exams. And to please go and water the plants outside, they were dying of thirst. It was very hot out. Hot and muggy. Like Morocco last summer when they were there with Alex and Desirée, and they had to stay in all day with the air conditioning on and lie around in those pretty Moroccan silk robes they found in the souk in Marrakesh, some with gold motifs, some with little bells hanging from the sleeves.

After Maria was done in the kitchen she started to make the beds. Strands of her hair got in her face, so she had to pause a moment in order to put her hair back up. She started putting the pins back in carefully and noticed she was sweating under her arms.

M. Bresson came in suddenly and surprised her. She didn't have time to put all the pins back in so her hair fell around her face and behind her ears and she felt embarrassed. She held the remaining pins in her hand as he talked. He joked about her always putting her hair back like that, why not leave it loose, it was so much nicer, but Maria told him, blushing, that it was not comfortable for work. M. Bresson said well, well, he understood that perfectly, it was nice to have someone who took her work seriously for a change, and what was all of this about a wedding, his wife told him she was getting married. Maria nodded her head gently and said yes, it was true, it was decided this morning at seven thirty. And M. Bresson said, indeed. Well, when would they be getting married? he asked her, and what did her fiancé do. Maria said they would be married in August, which was really soon, it was only two and a half months away. And there were so many things to prepare ... the dress, the meal, all of that. Her parents were happy though. She talked to them this morning. They were going to have the wedding at their house. It was big and it was in the country. M. Bresson said that was very nice and wished her the best. And, of course, she could have the whole month of August off, that went without saying. Maria said thank you very much, actually that was what she had wanted to talk about with Mme Bresson this morning, but there'd been so much to do she hadn't had the chance. M. Bresson told her she needn't worry, he would tell her himself. Then he left the room and she stuck the last pins back in her hair.

Usually around five o'clock the family would have tea. They would always offer Maria a cup, sometimes with a biscuit. She'd have it alone in Eric's old room (their married son who lived in England), and sometimes she'd even look through his old school books.

That day Mme Bresson offered her a slice of cake from behind the living-room door and whispered to her that, unfortunately, she couldn't talk because they had guests, but that she'd see her tomorrow at nine o'clock sharp. She wished her once again much happiness and reminded her about the clothes she had to pick up from the cleaner's before coming tomorrow, actually, it would be even better if she picked them up now and left them with the concierge, although, come to think of it, she could pick them up tomorrow, that would be fine.

As she was leaving, Maria heard them all laugh suddenly from the living room, and she overheard one of their guests mention that she and her husband were going to Cascais in Portugal that summer, they had rented a villa. Maria almost wanted to go back in and ask her about it, tell her she was from around there, but she knew she couldn't.

Two weeks later, Emma came back home with a man. She introduced him to Maria as Philippe and went with him into her bedroom. Maria suddenly felt very hot so she went into the kitchen to get herself a glass of water. Emma came back out half an hour later. Maria felt relieved.

Emma was very pretty. She had long blonde hair, green eyes, and always wore nice clothes. Sometimes she wore tight miniskirts and Maria told her she envied her legs.

She had entered university the previous year and was studying law. She often told Maria how bored she was with her studies, how all she wanted to do was go out and have fun, have her own apartment (with good luck by the end of the year) and never have to work. Maria listened carefully, never asking too many questions, nodding her head from time to time. Sometimes she'd tilt her head gently, her big eyes gazing inquisitively into Emma's, her mouth slightly open, her hands folded, like a Madonna from a Renaissance painting.

The same day Philippe came over, Maria tripped over the vacuum cleaner and hurt her knee. When she got up, she noticed it was bleeding so she went to the bathroom to put some alcohol on it. As she opened the door, she saw Emma and Philippe kissing in the shower. The water was pouring all over their bodies, there was steam everywhere and Philippe was caressing her insidiously. Maria slammed the door abruptly and ran, holding her knee in pain. Once again she felt hot all over, even nauseous, she was sweating and she felt like crying. She went into the kitchen where she cut off a piece of an old tea towel with oranges and pineapples printed on it, then poured some vinegar on to her wound, tied the towel around it and went to sit down on Eric's bed. It was only four thirty, she couldn't possibly leave until at least five o'clock, so she looked at one of Eric's books once again, moving her lips as she read.

Then she heard Emma calling her, so she quickly closed the book, arranged her hair and went back into the living room, where both of them were now dressed, their hair wet, smoking cigarettes.

Emma asked her if she wanted a cigarette. Maria hastily said no thank you, but then Emma smiled and told her not to be afraid, she wouldn't tell her mother, but she had seen Maria light a cigarette just the other day, as she was leaving the house. Then, as she was talking, she noticed the tea towel around Maria's knee and asked her what in the world had happened to her. Maria laughed awkwardly and said it was nothing really. But Philippe insisted on looking at it, told her he was a medical student, stuck a cigarette in the corner of his lip as he looked at it carefully and told her to go and disinfect it immediately.

She went to the bathroom, put some antiseptic and a Band-Aid on it and walked back to the living room, determined to accept a cigarette. But on the way she heard them laugh and became worried that it might be at her expense (maybe Philippe wasn't really a medical student, maybe he just said it to make fun of her), so instead she went to dust the candelabras that stood on the mantelpiece in M. and Mme Bresson's bedroom. As she was dusting, she heard Emma's footsteps in the hallway, they sounded squeakier and louder than usual, she had probably bought herself another pair of shoes.

At five o'clock, Maria went back into Eric's room and changed into her own clothes. She carefully folded her white uniform, and put her skirt and blouse back on. Her knee felt better and she started humming softly. Emma came in as she was about to leave and told her she wanted to know more about the wedding, all she had ever said to her was that she was getting married and that was it. She wanted to know more about Pablo, what he did, how they met, what he looked like.

Maria told her he was a little taller than she was, he had a thin moustache and green eyes, his hair was dark and curly and he was very muscular. Emma asked how come. Maria said it was because he carried a lot of heavy things in his job—

Emma interrupted her and asked her what Pablo did. Maria bent her head down a little bit and muttered something that Emma didn't hear so she had to say it a little bit louder. The red came back to her face as she told Emma that he was a builder.

Emma laughed and said it really wasn't that bad, why be so embarrassed about it, and Maria said she wasn't embarrassed, not at all, on the contrary.

Emma asked her again how they met. Maria said he was the son of a friend of her aunt Mariella, who lived in a tiny apartment in a dangerous area in Lisbon where it was frightening to go and visit her because the boys there followed girls and sometimes did horrible things to them, she even knew a girl to whom it had happened, the daughter of a friend of Mariella, but even that didn't make her move – Mariella, not the girl.

Mariella still lived there, in the tiny apartment with yellow wallpaper and eleven flowerpots. It always smelled good at Mariella's, like a garden, and that was where she had met Pablo – among the flowerpots. By then Maria had already moved to Paris, people looked at her differently, they were nicer to her so she felt more appreciated. It was an agreeable feeling, especially since Pablo seemed very interested, he asked her many questions about her new life abroad.

After she went back to Paris she got a letter from him saying he was coming there too, he didn't like living in Portugal any more, did she know of a place where he could stay.

That was one year ago. He moved into an apartment next to hers and they started going out together. Maria told Emma that he was the only boy she had ever known, she was a shy girl, she had never met anyone else. Boys were never interested in her. Pablo was the only one who had ever told her that he loved her. He was the one who wanted to get married, she could wait, but he didn't want to. He said he wanted to settle down and have children. Maria added that she didn't want children, at least not right now, getting married was frightening enough, she'd seen what it had done to her older sister Teresa, once she got married her husband stopped being as nice to her as he used to be, stopped buying her gifts and kissing her in public, he even grew a beard and got fatter, and now he ordered her around all the time, brought home friends from the business (he was a carpenter) and made her cook for all of them almost every night. She was so good she never said anything, never complained. When she was seven months pregnant she still went on cooking and cleaning for him like that, until one day she fainted on the kitchen floor and the doctor told her that if she went on exhausting herself like that she would lose her baby.

Emma told Maria that it was terrible indeed, but from what she had described, it didn't really sound as though Pablo would do the same thing, but Maria didn't reply. Instead, she scratched her arm, then her neck, leaving red marks on it. Then, her voice suddenly lower, Maria confessed that she was worried about living with a man, what if she decided she didn't like him any more, where would she go, what would she do? And what if she met somebody she liked more? Then she pressed her hand to her cheek and said she was so sorry for saying such things in front of her, so embarrassed. Emma told her not to be silly, it was normal to feel those things and to be nervous before getting married, everything would be all right, and Maria said yes, of course.

Then Maria added that the last time she went to visit her mother she was asked all kinds of questions about Pablo and was told that it was time she started to think seriously about getting married, didn't she remember what happened to her beautiful friend Sylvia Gonzales, who used to sleep around with many boys and when she got pregnant she didn't know who the father was so she had to retire in shame to the next-door village, where she gave birth to a little boy and nobody went to see her, not even her own mother, the woman who used to sell perfumes on the Costa del Paradiso and who now also lives in shame and never goes out, and they say she still puts on her make-up every day and her house smells like a rotten lily of the valley.

Then Maria laughed and said that even if she had wanted to be like Sylvia Gonzales she couldn't have because Sylvia was really beautiful, tall and thin, with blue eyes and boys were in love with her for as long as she could remember.

Emma told her not to talk like that, it was not because one was beautiful that boys fell in love with you, that was an old cliché, and Maria asked her what a cliché was.

Philippe came into the room and asked Emma where the cigarettes were, and winked at Maria as he went back out. She told Emma he was a very nice boy and asked if she was going to marry him. Emma laughed and said no, not at all. Maria remembered the way he had held her in the shower, she wanted to say something about it, but she didn't dare. So instead she asked Emma if she wanted to hear about the dress, and as she was talking her eyes were shining and she talked faster, moving her hands a lot, while she described the dress which would be made of satin and lace, with a long ribbon in the back. She would also have a little crown on her head, like a queen, and a woman was going to come specially to do her make-up.

After the wedding they would spend two nights in an old monastery on top of a mountain near Evora, did Emma know Evora, it was a beautiful place, always full of tourists. The next day they would go to the Algarve and stay there, but not with her sister. They would be back in Paris on August the thirtieth, and she'd be ready to start work again on September the first.

Emma said that sounded wonderful, wasn't she excited, it sounded so romantic. Maria told her Pablo was excited, he was very happy. Emma asked her if she was happy, and Maria said yes, of course, but she had to leave now, it was past five o'clock.

Emma left the room, and Maria looked at herself in the mirror, adjusted her hairpins one last time and, as she opened the door, heard Mme Bresson's voice in the hallway.

Is that you, Maria, asked Mme Bresson. Maria, is that you, would you please come here for one second before leaving, there's something I must ask you.

I'm coming, said Maria, and as she went into the kitchen she saw Mme Bresson moving her nostrils in an agitated way. What fell here, she asked her dryly, it smells of vinegar everywhere, anyway, I wanted to ask you if tomorrow morning before coming here you can stop by Merlaud, you know the butcher on the rue du Bac (they open at nine), and get me six slices of veal, I'm having guests for dinner. Maria said of course she would, and Mme Bresson smiled and told her she would see her tomorrow, here was the money for the veal, she could go now, but, oh yes, she mustn't forget about the butcher's receipt. Maria slipped the two hundred-franc notes in her pocket and asked Mme Bresson if she wanted her to wash the floor in order to get the vinegar out, it was true it smelled, she was very sorry it was her fault, she hurt her knee earlier so she put some vinegar on it to soothe the pain. Mme Bresson moved her nostrils again and said what kind of crude methods are those, she was not in Africa here, she was in Paris in a civilized home where they used antiseptics and not kitchen supplies to cure wounds. Maria stammered and said yes, she knew, but Emma had been in the bathroom and she didn't want to bother her, so instead she used the vinegar, her mother used to use it. Mme Bresson did not respond but went to find Emma who was saying goodbye to Philippe.

As Maria went to fetch her coat, she overheard Mme Bresson asking Emma about Philippe, saying he looked like a very nice boy, what did he do, what did his parents do. Emma said he studied painting, his father owned a funeral home and his mother was a drug addict. Mme Bresson sneered and said that wasn't funny at all, why didn't she go and study for a bit instead of having a different boyfriend every week and talking to the maid all day. Emma said excuse me but I'm twenty-two years old, I'm past the age where you can tell me what to do. I don't have a different boyfriend every week, and I don't always talk to the maid. Besides, she's very nice. The rest of the conversation was drowned out by the sound of running water, until Maria went into the kitchen to say goodbye to both of them. Mme Bresson was laughing, it was the first time in five years Maria had seen her laugh that way, she had two large dimples, her whole face was lit up, and her made-up eyes were stretched out in a smile.

Maria said goodbye very fast, but Emma said wait, wait, do you like red, I have a red shirt I never wear, come and take a look at it. Maria followed her into the room. She noticed that the sheets on the bed were creased and Emma's underwear was on the floor. She suddenly felt the same uncontrollable feeling coming over her again, the nausea, the heat shooting up in her body, the sweat forming on her forehead in a nest of tepid drops. She accepted the red shirt with trembling hands but suddenly the tears came back again, this time she couldn't keep them from falling. She covered her face with her two hands and dropped the shirt on the bed. Emma asked her disconcertedly what the matter was, why was she crying like that. Maria said she didn't know, she just felt very sad, she was so sorry, so embarrassed, she must get home soon and go and find a veil for the dress, a nice long veil that would cover her face and make everything look as if she was looking out of a clouded window.

Emma took her hand and said please don't cry, Maria, please. Then Mme Bresson called out, is everything all right? And Maria ran out of the room saying I'm sorry, I must go, and dried her tears quickly. Emma followed her saying Maria, Maria, but that was all she could say. Maria said I'm sorry, again, and left quickly.

As she waited for the elevator she took a little compact out of her purse and made sure her eyes were not red. She heard Mme Bresson on the phone, speaking loudly.

I'm so exhausted, she was saying, I've had such a hard day, between Emma and the maid, and Henri with all his problems and his bad temper, it's just too much. Too much. What are you doing tomorrow afternoon? We could go shopping, I need a dress for the reception on Friday evening, maybe something pink or green, what do you think, or maybe I'll just wear the same dress I wore last year at that party with Dominique and Lucien, you know, the party where that Italian man flirted with me, Giovanni was his name, that was so funny, he held me tight against his chest and told me I was so attractive – I didn't tell you that? Well he did. He held me so hard I couldn't breathe, and he smelled so good, it reminded me of the cologne my uncle used to wear when I was a little girl and he'd come and visit us in our house at the beach where the grown-ups used to play chess every night and the children used to howl at the moon, like wolves.

The elevator came. When Maria got in, she realized she had forgotten the red shirt. Pablo would have liked it on her; she would get it tomorrow. She looked at her hands which were red from all the scrubbing, they looked like her mother's hands, when she used to call the children for dinner, 'Janta! Janta!', and clap her hands methodically, one beat a syllable, like the sound of the plough the farmers used in the fields.

Wires

They sat around a round wooden table, drinking white wine and eating finger sandwiches. At one point it seemed that there was nothing else to say, so they remained silent for a short while, listening to their own breathing and chewing, their eyes wandering about the room, avoiding each other's glances.

'I'm going to call my answering machine again,' Lucy said, pushing her hair back and getting up.

'You just called it fifteen minutes ago,' Antonia said.

'So what? Maybe he called between now and then.'

'Go and call it then,' Yuri said impatiently.

Lucy was gone for about five minutes, during which time Yuri put his arm around Antonia's waist, and slid his hand underneath her dress. She pushed him away, laughing.

Yuri was very tall, with an imposing nose, vivacious blue eyes, thick dark hair and a seductive smile. He spoke loudly and laughed frequently, sometimes for no apparent reason. Antonia looked frail next to him, a short, blonde-haired woman with small bones and a beautiful, fragile face, reminiscent of an Ingres painting. That evening she was dressed in a pink linen dress, exposing her tanned legs and cleavage.

Yuri kissed his wife on the nape of her neck. He told her he was getting a little sick and tired of Lucy's neurosis.

Why did they have to invite her to the country, especially for five days, didn't they see enough of her in Paris? Also, she didn't need a vacation as much as he did, her whole life was a vacation, for Christ's sake. And not only that, but who cared about her life, it seemed so complicated, falling in love with someone different every five minutes, God, she was so obsessed, Jesus, how obsessed can you get.

'First of all,' Antonia replied, 'I always thought you liked Lucy. Second of all, when I asked you what you thought about the idea of having her and Irving over, you said great, let's fix them up. Do you remember?'

'Vaguely,' Yuri answered. 'Well, I suppose it would be nice if something happened between them.'

'I suppose so.'

'Lucy and Irving. Maybe he'll be able to take her mind off that imbecile she keeps calling.'

'I doubt it,' Antonia said, 'and even if he could, I don't think Lucy is interested in him in the least. And I can see why,' she added, smiling softly.

'Why do you say that? Irving is a wonderful man, a loyal friend. He could be good for her.'

At the same moment Irving came into the room and asked them if they wanted to go out on to the porch for some martinis. He was overweight, with a salt and pepper beard, cracked lips and gentle eyes.

'I need a drink,' he announced. 'One of my characters just got killed, the housekeeper discovered him dead in the bathtub. I can't believe I'm actually writing this kind of crap. Where's Lucy?'

'On the phone again.' Yuri sighed. 'I come to the South

of France to relax, after four months of shooting that ludicrous movie, and what do I get . . . ?

'I need to call my agent,' Irving said. 'She'd better not take too long.'

'Don't worry about her taking too long,' Yuri said sarcastically as Lucy came back in, her cheeks flushed. She was a very attractive woman in her late twenties, with porcelain-like skin, long auburn hair and a thin, angular body. She walked gracefully, her feet barely touching the ground, her eyes looking downwards. She wore a coloured silk skirt, flared around the knees, and a white shirt, the first three buttons of which she had left undone.

'So?' Antonia asked.

'Nothing,' Lucy muttered. 'What time is it?'

'It's one minute and thirty-two seconds after you called him last,' Yuri joked.

'Very funny,' Lucy retorted.

'Personally I tend to think it's hilarious. Don't you, Irving?'

'Oh, I don't know,' Irving said uncomfortably. 'I'll see you outside.'

'Yuri, I can just imagine what you say about me when I'm not here,' Lucy said. 'You really have it in for me, don't you? I mean you think I'm behaving like a child over this guy, don't you? Well, maybe I am. But is it any of your goddamn business? No. And do I care what you think? No.'

'So why are you even bringing it up?' Yuri asked.

'Yuri, Lucy,' Antonia said, 'come on, both of you . . .'

'He hates me,' Lucy said. 'Your husband hates me.'

'I don't hate you,' Yuri said, 'you know very well I don't hate you. On the contrary, I'm enjoying every minute of this, it's like being on a set again.'

'Is it really?' Lucy snapped. 'Well, I'm so glad I can entertain you in that way.'

'God, Lucy, you're so touchy,' Yuri said, waving his hand dismissively.

'Come on, come out for some martinis,' Irving called out.

'Your agent,' Yuri said.

'What?'

'Your agent. You said you have to call your agent.'

'Oh, I'll do it later. I need a drink first.'

They all went out on to the porch and marvelled at the beauty of the landscape, rows and rows of lush green hills, a white half-moon lurking from behind the trees. The ivy-covered stone house stood imposingly against this lovely backdrop, its blue painted shutters flapping in the wind, and the half-open front door, a rusty wooden one, creaking incessantly.

'This is my favourite hour,' Antonia said in a dreamy voice. 'Twilight. It's also one of my favourite French words. Crépuscule. Isn't it beautiful?'

'I hate it,' Yuri said, 'it reminds me of a cracker. Crac. Croc.'

'You're so difficult,' Antonia sighed. 'Why did I have to marry such a difficult man, why?'

'Because you love me,' Yuri said, taking hold of her and giving her a wet kiss, 'and I love you.'

'Jesus,' Irving said, looking ill at ease.

'Don't say "Jesus",' Antonia said, her face buried in Yuri's shoulder, her arms around his waist. 'Why don't you pour us some martinis, Irving?'

'Oh, martinis, mar-ti-tinis,' Yuri sang, as he pretended to waltz with Antonia.

'I love it here,' Irving said as he poured the drinks. 'I'm so happy you bought the house, really this is the best thing you could have done, buying a country house in Provence. God, what else do you need in life! Look at this landscape, this peace, the smells, it's all so perfect . . .'

'Except for the French,' Yuri said. 'I hate the French.'

'And you've been living here for twenty-five years and you have a French wife . . .' Irving sighed.

'We have to get that front door fixed,' Antonia muttered.

'What?' Yuri asked.

'The front door. It needs to be fixed. It never stops creaking.'

'Well, what are you waiting for? You've been complaining about that door for two years,' Yuri remarked petulantly.

'What am I waiting for? What about you? Did it ever occur to you that you should take care of it?' Antonia snapped back.

'No, my dear, it did not, for the mere reason that the creak of that door does not bother me in the least. On the contrary, I rather enjoy it.'

'God, Antonia, how can you deal with him . . .' Lucy mumbled.

'Come on, all of you, let's not talk about this any more,' Irving pleaded, 'it's totally insignificant. Let's get back to the French instead. What were we saying about the French?'

Yuri shrugged his shoulders. 'That we can't live without them. Without their complaining, without their contempt for the outside world . . .'

'Well, I like the French,' Lucy interceded.

'Is that so?' asked Yuri, taking a loud sip of his martini.

'Well, you must like something about them since you married a French woman,' Lucy answered dryly.

'I'm not typically French,' Antonia announced firmly.

'Very true, my dear,' Yuri acquiesced, although not without a note of irony in his voice. 'Antonia is not typically French. It's the typical French, the "Français moyen", I'm talking about.'

'Why are you living here then?' Lucy asked.

'Because France was the only country to grant me asylum when I left Russia twenty-five years ago. I owe them what I am today. Without them who knows where I'd be right now. Probably dead or in a Siberian camp. They didn't like my outspokenness over there. Here they think it's so very "charmant".'

'Do you feel like this is your home?'

'I don't know,' Yuri answered. 'I've been thrown out of my country and I'm a Jew. I feel like I'm in exile wherever I am.'

'That's interesting,' Lucy said thoughtfully, 'that's very interesting. I wonder if European Jews feel that way more than American Jews.'

'I couldn't say,' Yuri answered, 'I'm not an American Jew. Ask Irving. How do you feel about that, Irving?'

'I belong to Los Angeles and that's all there is to it.'

Irving laughed. 'No other home for me than Malibu Beach and Sunset Boulevard!'

'Well,' Lucy declared, getting up to pour herself another drink, 'I'm beginning to feel as if Paris is my second home. I often hear Americans speak, in cafés, in restaurants, and it all of a sudden hits me that I share the same culture and language as these people, and that concept just blows me away. I mean I feel so different from them, you know?'

'I know what you mean,' Antonia said sympathetically.

'No, really. I feel very removed from that side of the Atlantic. I have a nicer apartment and my design work took off better here than it ever did in New York.'

They heard a car park in the driveway and Antonia adjusted her hair. 'That's probably Claire and Ludovic. I told them to come for drinks.'

'Thanks for telling me,' Yuri grumbled. 'Who the hell are Claire and Ludovic?'

'I hope they speak English,' Irving said, 'because I don't have to remind you that I don't speak a word of French.'

'No, you don't have to remind us.' Yuri sighed.

'Claire and Ludovic are two people I met a couple of nights ago at Henri's,' Antonia explained. 'Oh, come on, Yuri, you invite people without telling me all the time.'

'Fine, fine . . .' He settled into a wicker armchair and crossed his legs, as Antonia and Irving went to greet the guests.

'Lucy, come sit next to me,' he said, patting the chair next to him. She sat down, stretching her long white legs which glowed in the dim evening light. She blushed as she caught him looking at her legs.

'So, tell me about this guy,' Yuri said matter of factly. 'Are you in love with him?'

'Why do you ask?' she said, surprised.

'I don't know, I was just wondering,' he said.

'Well, yes, as a matter of fact, I think I am,' she answered gravely. 'I'm experiencing a mixture of love and fear, since one doesn't go without the other.'

'And what about him? Do you think he loves you? What does he say to you? How does he act with you in bed?'

'God, Yuri, what a question ... Why do you want to know?' she laughed nervously.

'I'm trying to picture what it might feel like to be in love with you.' He lit a cigarette and furrowed his brow.

'Oh,' she said simply.

'Well,' Yuri laughed, 'I guess that comment doesn't quite make sense, does it. And anyway there's only one way to find out, isn't there ...'

She sighed loudly and avoided his gaze.

'I'm sorry, Lucy, I was just being crude, that's all,' he said, patting her bare knee.

She smiled meekly. 'I hope so,' she answered, crossing her legs and covering her knees with her flowery silk skirt.

'So,' he said, taking a sip of his martini, 'let's get back to our little friend here. Is he or isn't he in love with you?'

'I don't really want to talk about it,' Lucy said. 'And besides, he's not so little, he's your age.'

'Is he really?' Yuri appeared surprised. 'Well, in that case he must be in love with you,' he added, smiling.

'God, Yuri, will you give me a break?' she said, trying to conceal a flattered smile.

'Fine,' Yuri said, putting his drink down abruptly, 'so let's talk about something else. Let me see . . .' He creased his brow and held his chin in his left hand. 'Let me see . . .' he repeated. 'Ah! Here we go. A good subject of conversation. You tell me and I'll tell you. How many men have you slept with in your life? Less than twenty or more than thirty? Or somewhere in between?'

'Please,' she moaned, 'not that.'

'Why not? It's an interesting topic.'

'Okay, fine, so if you really want to know, no, he's not in love with me,' Lucy said slowly.

'Finally, we're getting somewhere. Now. Why do you think he's not in love with you?'

'He's not in love with me,' she said, 'because he's too independent. He doesn't have time to think about anybody. But that's okay, I guess.'

'Aha, I see. So you're saying that because he won't compromise, this means he's not in love with you?'

'Exactly. And until he can show me that he's willing to make compromises, to be more demonstrative, I will continue to keep my distance.'

'And what if he's actually waiting for you to make compromises? For you to warm up to him?'

'I don't know . . . I never thought about it that way. And knowing the guy, I don't think that's the case.'

'So you're saying the guy is basically a cold fish with an umbrella stuck up his ass—'

'Do you always have to be so fucking rude, Yuri?' Lucy flared her nostrils and gave Yuri a condescending glance which he returned with an exaggerated smile.

'Men are wolves, Lucy,' he said. 'They get tired of their

prey very quickly. Playing games only works for a short while, until it loses its appeal. And when that happens, we run away. Not before having a last little bite of you, of course, because we like to take full advantage of the situation before saying "bye bye!"' he added in a jovial tone, to which Lucy reacted with a look of disdain on her face.

'You are so vile, Yuri, it's beyond belief. Just gross.'

'But it's so much fun being vile with you, Lucy,' he said, putting his arm around her and kissing the nape of her neck. 'So, how shall I put it, enticing . . .'

'Stop it, Yuri!' she shouted, pushing his arm away. 'You're starting to really get on my nerves.'

'Fine, forget it. I'm just trying to protect you from the big wild wolves out there. There's nothing wrong with being honest with men, you know. Earnest, certainly not, but honest, absolutely.'

'Thanks for the advice, I'll think about it. Can we talk about something else now, you Russian swine?'

Yuri burst out laughing. 'I love it when you insult me. That's the way you should talk to those suitors of yours. Give them hell. They'll come panting to your feet.'

'They won't. I've tried it. I told you. It's better to be cold and distant. It's just as good as insulting them, and at least that way you don't appear callous or insane, which is exactly the way you appear to be.'

'I find your vulnerability so arousing,' Yuri commented, a flirtatious smile on his face, 'and I want to make a deal with you. Once you do meet the right man in your life, which I'm sure you will, I'd be interested in seeing if your theories are still relevant. If they are I will rest my case.'

Lucy rolled her eyes. 'Please.'

'No, I'm serious.'

'All right. And if they're no longer relevant?'

'I will chide you about it for the rest of your life.'

'People are allowed to change, you know,' Lucy said softly.

'Indeed they are,' he answered, looking at her in a perplexed way.

Irving appeared, holding a few magazines. 'Hi, folks,' he said, 'what's up?'

'Lucy's teaching me all about her love life. What it basically comes down to, is, be as hard as a rock and don't let men see through you. Until, of course, they get fed up with trying to figure you out and they go on to warmer and more exciting things. Large breasts, milky thighs, women who can never get enough of it—'

'You're such a horny pig, Yuri. I don't know how Antonia puts up with you. Actually, I don't even want to *think* about how she puts up with you. The thought just horrifies me. And to set the record straight, all I said was at the beginning of a relationship it's better if you don't expose yourself too much. You call that vulnerability, I call it common sense. All we're talking about here is a guy I see once or twice a week, and for the moment that satisfies me plenty.'

'Yet you're going crazy waiting for his phone call,' Irving added. 'You call that satisfaction?'

'I can't get no –' Yuri started singing loudly '– satisfaction—'

'Shut up,' Irving muttered.

'Louis and I are supposed to go see *Samson and Delila*

132

together at the opera,' Lucy ventured, as if oblivious to Yuri and Irving. 'And that's why I need to talk to him.'

'Is that what he's called, Louis?' Yuri asked.

'No, I just kind of made that up,' Lucy retorted dryly.

'And assuming he does call you, what about calling you just for the sake of finding out how you are?' Irving asked in an impatient tone of voice.

'He won't,' she answered firmly, 'he doesn't care about me in that way. He doesn't bother with unnecessary words.'

'Is asking how you are unnecessary?' Irving asked.

'Ha,' Yuri said.

'We have the greatest sex,' she said.

Yuri looked at her inquisitively. 'Do you really?' he asked. 'What techniques does he use?'

'Anything from the Kama Sutra,' Lucy retorted.

'You two are terrible. And I need some chapstick, my lips are dry,' Irving interrupted. 'The main character in my script was just murdered in his bathtub. Like Marat.'

'You told us that before,' Yuri said. He bent over towards Lucy, winked at her and said, 'Irving doesn't like to talk about sex.' Both he and Lucy started laughing.

'Shut up,' Irving said again.

'Oh, come on, Irving,' Lucy said gently. 'Actually I have to go make a phone call. And no, it's not him this time, but my mother.'

'Your mother,' Yuri snarled. 'Can I dial the number for you and say hello? I haven't spoken to her in ages. And please feel free to call America long distance from my phone, it only costs something like five hundred francs a minute . . .'

'I'll call her collect,' Lucy answered, before walking away.

'Why don't you just dump the guy?' Yuri raised his voice. 'It's time you found someone more solid than that.'

Lucy slammed the door.

'I wonder who that solid person might be . . .' Irving mumbled.

'I beg your pardon?' Yuri asked.

'Never mind,' Irving answered, 'all I mean is you didn't have to mention that dumping stuff, it wasn't very nice.'

'I know I didn't, but I wanted to. She drives me nuts this girl, calling this idiot every five minutes. Anyhow, he's probably screwing someone else as we speak.'

'She's beautiful,' Irving whispered.

'Why are you whispering it?' Yuri asked impudently.

'I don't know.' Irving fidgeted with his glass and looked at Yuri. 'Why are you always so goddamn abrasive?'

'I'm not abrasive. I'm just noticing certain things about you, that's all.'

'Yeah? Like what?'

'Drop it. It's really not very important.'

'No. Let's not drop it. What are you noticing about me that you didn't notice before? That I'm not suave enough, like you? That I'm not as crude and perverted as you are? I'm no fool, Yuri. I know what's going on in your head. You want to fuck her and that's all there is to it. You can't deny it. It shows on your face. And if you want to know the truth, I find it particularly disgusting.' His voice rose sharply and Yuri put his hand on his shoulder.

'Come on, Irving, relax. You don't know what you're talking about. Really, it's not worth getting so angry.'

'Yeah, right.'

'I'm sorry about what I said before, okay? Now. L'affaire est close, as they say in French. Let's forget about it. Where's Antonia?'

'I don't know. She's talking to her friends. I think they're in the kitchen.'

He got up abruptly, threw the magazines on the floor and walked away talking to himself.

'Antonia!' Yuri hollered, 'Antonia!'

She appeared with Claire and Ludovic, a shy-looking and well-dressed short couple who held hands as they stood and talked. Irving came back out almost immediately, his hair wet and water dripping from his face.

'God, Irving,' Antonia observed, 'what happened to you, you're all wet. Anyway, this is Claire, this is Ludovic. Ludovic, this is my husband, Yuri – Claire, Yuri – Yuri, Claire.'

'Hello,' they said in unison.

'I like your work very much,' Ludovic said in thickly accented English to Yuri, 'I've seen almost every film you've been in.'

'You have? My God . . . Even I haven't seen all the films I've been in.'

'Yuri,' Antonia warned. 'Would you all like some martinis? Or some wine?'

'Oh, some wine for me,' Claire said. She wore a rather severe black suit with a white polka-dot handkerchief stuck in the side pocket and her dark hair was combed into a perfect braid.

'I'll have some wine too,' Ludovic replied, finally letting go of her hand.

Lucy came back out.

'So?' Irving asked.

'Nothing. But I left a message on his machine, saying he should call here tonight or tomorrow morning.'

She sat down and didn't bother to introduce herself to the newcomers. She bent her head down, staring at the ground, her elbows on her knees.

'The shithead isn't going to call,' she finally said. 'And you know what?'

'What?' Antonia asked.

'I don't care.'

'Of course you don't.' Yuri burst out laughing.

'What's so funny?' Irving asked, looking distraught. 'Did I miss something?'

'Who knows what's so funny.' Antonia shrugged her shoulders. 'He's drunk. At least he's laughing, let him laugh.'

'He's always laughing,' Lucy said.

'Is anybody hungry?' Antonia asked.

'I am,' Irving said, patting his stomach.

'I'm not,' Yuri said, 'especially not after all those sandwiches . . .'

'Excuse me, but I think I hear the telephone,' Ludovic ventured timidly.

Lucy leaped up and ran into the house, only to come back immediately. 'Irving, it's for you, it's Blossom.'

He lifted himself heavily out of his chair and disappeared into the house.

'Feminism is a lost cause,' Lucy said, 'look at me waiting for the goddamn phone to ring.'

'Are you expecting an important phone call?' Claire asked in a heavy French accent.

'Yes,' Lucy said, trying to sound friendly. 'You know. *That* kind of a phone call.'

'Oh,' said Claire, looking a little perplexed.

'She's waiting for her boyfriend to call,' Antonia explained.

Claire's mouth opened into a wide smile. 'I understand very well,' she said sympathetically, 'it is a difficult thing. I don't have to worry about this because now I am married.'

She proudly stuck a slim, tanned hand out. 'This is a diamond, this is a sapphire,' she said, pointing towards an imposing ring which stood majestically upon her fourth finger. 'Ludovic bought it for me in Rome while I was waiting for him in a café. I waited and waited, all these men were bothering me, you know how it is in Italy, and when he finally arrived all sweating, you know, he asked me to marry him and I was so angry with him because he made me wait that I said no. Then, of course, he pulled this ring out and I had to say yes.' She laughed, a charming laugh, showing a perfect set of white teeth.

'How sweet,' Lucy said, attempting a sympathetic smile. 'And how long have you been married for?'

'Eight months,' Claire said, smiling happily. 'You should come and see our house.'

'That sounds nice,' said Lucy, in a feeble voice.

'I'm tired,' Antonia said to no one in particular.

'Come here,' Yuri said, seating her on his lap and putting his strong arms around her.

A sudden stillness enveloped them as the moon

emerged fully from behind the hills. The wind started blowing frantically, drowning out Irving's voice in the background. They shivered and hugged their arms together for a long time before getting up and entering the house, their heads lowered as if they were all about to be sentenced for some unspeakable crime.

Later on, after Claire and Ludovic were gone, they sat at the same candlelit wooden table, eating roast chicken and potatoes with thick gravy.

'I should have invited them for dinner,' Antonia said, 'it wasn't nice of me.'

'What, are you crazy?' Yuri said, his mouth full. 'Those two yuppies?'

'They're not yuppies,' Antonia objected vehemently. 'And even if they were, so what? They're young, nice, innocent people who were just trying to be civil and right away you criticize them. I just won't invite anyone again, that's all. And I wish you'd stop being so negative about everybody and everything.'

'I only want the best,' Yuri said, stuffing a whole potato in his mouth. 'I don't have time for mediocrity. I'm getting old. And the older I get, the more I hate compromises.'

'Do I have to remind you that you're not even forty-five?' Irving asked.

The phone rang again. 'I'll get it,' Lucy said casually.

'I'll get the salad,' Antonia said, wiping her mouth with her napkin before getting up.

'Yuri!' Lucy called out, 'it's for you!'

'Whoever it is, I'll call back!' he yelled.

Lucy glided slowly back into the room, a tragic look on

her face. She sat down delicately and interlaced her slender freckled fingers.

'Don't worry, he'll call,' Irving said, giving her an affectionate tap on the back.

'Lucy, do you know what Irving said about you before?' Yuri said smiling. 'Irving said a very nice thing about you.'

'Did you, Irving?' Lucy asked, looking surprised. 'What did you say?'

'Jesus,' Irving said, colour mounting to his face, 'you say one word and I'm leaving this table immediately. And I'm not kidding.'

'Oh, Irving, don't be so uptight,' Yuri said. 'Women love hearing these sort of things.'

'I'm telling you, I'm not kidding,' Irving threatened, his lips looking more cracked than ever.

'But don't you realize you're making this into a big deal? It's such a simple, innocent thing!'

Irving pushed his chair back loudly and banged his fist on the table. 'You're going too far, Yuri. I said shut the fuck up!' His cheeks were now bright red.

'Fine, I won't say anything,' Yuri capitulated, 'but I think you're crazy.'

Irving sat back down, but it took a while before he was able to regain his composure.

'I don't want any salad,' he said, as Antonia offered him some.

Yuri shook his head, amused. 'Come on, Irving, it's over. What did Blossom say?'

'Nothing special.'

'Oh, come on, Irving, get over it. What did she say?'

'Just that they want me back in LA. I'm going to go

back there before next week, they want me to rewrite the last part of my other script.'

'I'm so happy I don't live in the States any more, I never want to go back,' Lucy said, playing around with a salad leaf. 'What's your script about?' she added half-heartedly.

'Oh, it's a long story . . . Besides, it's boring.'

Since no one commented on this last remark, Irving didn't pursue the topic. Antonia attempted to smile, and the phone rang again.

This time Lucy got up without a word, and as she was dashing into the next room it stopped suddenly.

'I *know* that was him,' she exclaimed. 'I know it.'

'Nice guy,' Irving said.

'Come on, leave her alone,' Antonia said. 'Can't you see the poor girl is under a lot of stress?'

Lucy sat down. 'It's true, I am under a lot of stress,' she said, taking evident pleasure in the fact that she was labelled as such.

'I heard a remarkable story today,' Antonia said, her face shining in the candlelight. 'I heard it from Henri's wife, you know, the one who used to be married to Mazin.'

'She was married to Mazin?' Yuri appeared surprised.

'Who's Mazin?' Irving asked.

'A big film critic,' Antonia said. 'Anyway,' she continued, 'his wife, I mean Henri's wife, Jeanne, a charming woman, told me this story. Her best friend is a young woman named Geraldine. The reason I'm telling you this, by the way, is because I bumped into Jeanne at the supermarket this morning.'

'Did you buy tissue paper? We're out of tissue paper,' Yuri interrupted.

'Yes,' Antonia replied impatiently. 'Anyway, she was buying food for Geraldine since she's supposed to be arriving tomorrow and she wants to throw a big party in her honour and we're invited. And without my asking her she started telling me this woman's life story. She said that up until three years ago, Geraldine had been living with a man she was madly in love with, a brilliant philosopher named Marc. Everything was going very well between them until suddenly one morning, he left her.'

'Couldn't have been going that well,' Lucy remarked.

'Well,' Antonia continued, 'she was so devastated she tried to commit suicide. He didn't even come to see her when she was recovering in a hospital room. He just sent a note saying he never wanted to see her again. It was terrible.

'After a while, though, she tried to pull herself together. She had been on the verge of finishing her doctorate, and she tried with all her might to overcome her pain and go on with her work, but she wasn't able to do it. All she could think of night and day was him, that jerk who left her.'

'Maybe he had good reasons to,' Yuri said, 'you don't know the other side of the story.'

'Maybe she was too demanding,' Lucy ventured, 'maybe she wanted too much from him.'

'Maybe he was a schmuck,' Irving argued, 'maybe he was a self-absorbed intellectual who spent his days wondering why he was there with her and making her feel guilty about it.'

'Okay, fine, but the story isn't over. After two years, she finally started to recover, slowly but surely, going out with friends again, finally getting her doctorate, moving into a new apartment in the Bastille. And since she had put on a substantial amount of weight during those two years, she decided to take jazz dancing classes in order to get into shape. And remember, during all that time she hadn't met anyone she even remotely liked, and wasn't approached by anyone for that matter.'

'That's because men can sense when you're not available,' Lucy said. 'It discourages them.'

'Some men don't care if you're available or not, they go for it anyway,' Yuri objected, playing with his cigarette lighter.

'How would you know?' Antonia exclaimed.

'Please,' Yuri said, 'I had a life before you, remember?' He looked at Lucy who turned her head away.

'Let's not go through that one again,' Antonia said, 'we all know you were a playboy and bla bla bla.'

'I wish I had been a playboy...' Irving sighed, 'but I never had such luck. How did you do it, Yuri? What does it take?'

'How did I do it? I don't know how I did it. You tell him, Antonia. What does it take?'

'Please,' Antonia sighed, 'this conversation is going nowhere.'

'Go on with your story,' Lucy said, 'it's more interesting.'

'What's the matter, Lucy, you're not fascinated by me any more?' Yuri enquired flirtatiously, as Irving mumbled something under his breath.

Lucy declined to answer. 'Go on, Antonia,' she repeated, 'go on with your story.'

'Well,' Antonia continued, giving them both an inquisitive look, 'Geraldine started going to these dance classes, at first once, then twice, then three times a week. It got to the point where Jeanne started getting suspicious: how come she was getting this sudden burst of energy? Had she met anyone? Was she in love? So she confronted her. She told her she hoped she was in good health, it was certainly nice to see her enjoying life again, how did she like her dance classes? Geraldine blushed, looked very ill at ease, and told her she had something to confess.'

Antonia paused to take a sip of her wine.

'What did she tell her?' Lucy asked.

'She told her she was in love with her dance teacher,' Yuri said, lighting a cigarette. 'It's perfectly clear.'

'Shut up, Yuri,' Antonia said sharply.

The phone rang again and this time Irving picked it up. He came back smiling. 'It's for you, Lucy. I think it's him.'

'*Don't* finish the story until I'm back,' she said, running into the other room.

'Don't take more than an hour,' Yuri yelled from across the room.

Antonia and Irving started clearing the table and Yuri went to put on some music.

'I love the way this house smells,' Irving said as he helped her put the dishes into the dishwasher. 'Even though we're in the middle of June it still smells of winter. You know, dry leaves, charcoal, ivy . . .'

'Believe me,' Antonia said, 'I would live here all year

long if I could. But with Yuri, his work, his travelling, it's impossible. At least we have the house. I can't complain. Pass me the coffee, will you, I'm going to make a fresh pot.'

'You know,' Irving said, grabbing a large bag of coffee beans and pouring them into the grinder, 'I hope Lucy will be okay. She's such a nice girl and that guy sounds like such a creep . . .'

'Of course she'll be okay! She's much stronger than you think she is, you'd be surprised. I've known Lucy for a long time and she's always gotten over things faster than anyone I know. And believe me, she's gone through a lot.'

Lucy drifted into the kitchen, her cheeks flushed and her green eyes shining brightly.

'So?' Irving and Antonia asked at the same time.

'We didn't talk much. He said we're still on for Sunday night, it's raining in Paris and he misses me. It's the first time he's ever told me he misses me. It's all I needed to hear, I don't care about the rest any more.'

'Boy, if that's all it takes . . .' Irving muttered.

'Well, that's the way I am. It takes little to make me happy and little to make me sad.'

'I guess so . . . But tell me, how was he when he talked to you? Was he nice?'

'He was as he always is. Direct.'

'But was he nice, though? Or was he cold? Distant? I mean, don't you want somebody a little more caring, a little more tender?'

'Irving, I don't know what you're trying to get at but this is getting out of control!' she exclaimed. 'I mean, why would you care so much?'

'Forget it,' Irving apologized. 'You're right, it's none of my business.'

'That's right,' she said, walking quickly out of the kitchen and into the living room where Yuri had spread out a stack of records on the wine-coloured carpet.

'I don't know what to put on,' he said. 'What would you prefer, jazz or classical?'

'Classical,' she answered, kneeling down next to him and looking through his collection. 'Here,' she said, holding a dusty album cover, 'put this on. *Les nuits d'été*. It's so appropriate, and I love Berlioz.'

'Do you really?' Yuri seemed surprised.

'Yes, why? Is there anything wrong with liking Berlioz?'

'Not at all. It's just that you seem more like a Bryan Ferry type of girl—'

'And what's that supposed to mean?' Lucy interjected.

'Don't get so defensive,' he said gently. 'It's just that you happen to have chosen a piece I particularly love.'

Lucy blushed and started twirling her hair. 'How long have you and Antonia been married? Six or seven years?'

'Six. Why do you ask?'

'I don't know ... You just seem so happy together. I mean, especially after all the, you know, unfortunate things you both went through.'

'You mean the miscarriages? They're not things, Lucy. They're called miscarriages. You don't need to be afraid of saying it. It's okay now, we've learned how to deal with the situation.'

'That's good. I don't think you should ever give up hope. Your dream might be fulfilled one day.'

Yuri didn't answer and they remained silent, listening

to the music, until Irving and Antonia came back into the room.

'What's up, Lucy?' Irving asked cheerfully.

She sighed heavily and closed her eyes.

They sat back down at the table, waiting for the coffee to finish brewing. As the soprano's voice rose into a high crescendo, Irving said something none of them could hear.

'What?' Antonia yelled.

'It's too loud!' Irving shouted. 'Why don't you turn it down a little?'

Yuri got up lazily, a cigarette dangling from his lips.

'What happened to Geraldine?' Irving asked.

'Yes,' Lucy repeated, 'what happened to the girl?'

'Well,' Antonia said, leaning back in her chair and smoothing her hair, 'I'm sorry to say that she actually did fall in love with her dance teacher.'

'Ha, what did I say,' Yuri said.

'Yes, except that the dance teacher was a woman. She fell madly in love with her. She never said a word to her, not even hello. It lasted a year and a half. Wrote her anonymous letters, sent her presents, behaved as though she was really with her. Not only that, but it showed on her face. She looked and acted like somebody who's in love. Except that in her case it was all in her head. She ended up telling close friends about it, talking about the woman as if she truly were her lover. 'I'm sure Natasha would love this place,' she'd say if they went out to a restaurant; or 'Natasha would love this movie.' One day, it got to the point where Jeanne felt her friend was literally going crazy. She and Geraldine were having coffee, when suddenly Geraldine burst out crying and said, 'I have to break up with her, this can't go on.' Jeanne said, 'But you're not even together.' And Geraldine, amidst her tears, said, 'Yes, we are, but she doesn't know it.'

'My God,' Irving gasped, 'she really did go nuts, didn't she.'

Antonia shook her head. 'No. It finally ended. Geraldine went to see a psychoanalyst and since then she's a new woman. At least according to Jeanne she is. She's back to men again, although she hasn't met a man she likes; hopefully that will be the next step.'

'Irving,' Yuri said in a teasing tone of voice, 'how would you like to be responsible for someone's next step in life?'

'Don't answer him, Irving,' Antonia said, looking straight at Yuri.

'Fine. Nobody likes my jokes. So let's get serious then. Everyone seems to like being serious around here. So, I've got a question for all of you: why is it that they all end up going through analysis?'

'Who's they?' Lucy asked.

'People. Sad people. Distressed people. Lost people. Ordinary people. They all end up on the couch, as if that's the only remedy to their unhappiness.'

'Well, maybe it is, at least for some. What other remedy can you think of?' Irving asked. 'I don't know what I'd do without my shrink; he's my alter ego.'

'Christ,' Lucy said.

'I don't know,' Yuri said, looking puzzled and taking a long drag on his cigarette. 'In the nineteenth century people didn't ask themselves questions the way we do. They took themselves for granted. They weren't half as neurotic as we are now. They lived the way they had to live, in harsh and difficult conditions, and if they had a problem they dealt with it pragmatically and not emotionally. Look at us in comparison. We're spoilt and we're presented with so many choices – panaceas. Do you think those people had any choices back then? Yes, one: you deal on your own or you die. If you were a lucky person, you counted your blessings. We're never happy, there's always something wrong, and we only realize too late how lucky we are.'

'I'm not so sure,' Lucy said. 'How do you know that in the nineteenth century people didn't suffer as well? At least today we can proclaim our thoughts out loud, whereas back then one couldn't. People must have been much more repressed.'

'I hate that modern psychoanalytical term. It's over-used,' Yuri said, frowning.

'I think it's a great word,' Lucy replied. 'It clearly shows the disparity between what we think and what we say: that is, we don't always say what we think and we suffer from what we can't say.'

Irving yawned. 'I'm getting tired, I think I'll be heading upstairs.'

Antonia remained silent, fidgeting nervously, staring at the table.

'What the matter, Antonia?' Lucy asked. 'You look sad.'

She lifted her head up. 'Don't any of you care about that story I told you? Aren't you moved by my story?' She spoke more and more vehemently. 'Aren't you struck by the fact that this girl was able to create a whole relationship in her head and was actually cured by it? Don't you find that remarkable? Or are you all too goddamn self-centred to even see the importance of it? And that goes for all of you. *All* of you.'

'What's the matter with you?' Yuri shouted. 'Of course we're all self-centred! And please, no hysterics. I hate hysterics.'

'Shut up!' Antonia shouted back. 'Just because I'm moved by something it means I'm hysterical? Is that right? Why did I marry you, you selfish pig? How could I?!' She sent the pepper shaker flying across the table and ran out of the room followed by Yuri as Irving and Lucy sat speechless.

'I . . . I think I'll be going upstairs, these fights don't agree with me,' Irving said in a faint voice. He walked away, his heavy footsteps resonating on the staircase.

Lucy got up slowly and carried the coffee cups into the kitchen. She tied her hair into a ponytail and adjusted her skirt. Then, as she was about to make her way upstairs, she saw Yuri leaning against the hallway wall, staring at her.

'Antonia is very upset,' he said to her. 'But don't take any of this personally, it's all to do with me. She's sorry she even involved any of you.'

'I know,' Lucy answered, 'I didn't take it personally, although I think Irving might have.'

'He'll get over it. By tomorrow morning everybody will have forgotten about it. All this because of that stupid story.'

'It wasn't a stupid story,' Lucy argued, 'it was very interesting. To think that love can destroy you that way . . .' She shook her head, avoiding Yuri's piercing glance.

'I suppose that means you would never let yourself be destroyed by someone, manipulated to the point of losing your own self—'

'Well, you never know with these things, but no, I don't think so.' She laughed nervously.

A heavy silence lay between them. Lucy clumsily buttoned the three top buttons of her blouse, her cheeks suddenly red.

'Why did you just do that?' Yuri asked, lighting a cigarette.

'Why did I just do what?' she asked, her voice quivering.

'Why did you just button your blouse like that?' He kept his eyes fixed on hers, his legs crossed, his lips curved into a vague smile.

'I don't know . . . I'm . . . I'm cold,' she muttered, 'and I'm going to sleep. Goodnight.'

Yuri walked over to her, and delicately put his hand on her shirt. She swallowed hard as he unbuttoned those same buttons with unnerving slowness and dexterity, his breath against her neck, his hair softly brushing her face. She felt his fingers lightly touch her collarbone, sending a shiver down her spine. Then, he looked at her and smiled.

'There, that's much better now.'

He turned around and walked away slowly as she remained motionless, the touch of his fingers still warm against her skin. She thought she saw him turn around as he was walking up the stairs, but then again she wasn't sure; so she went up to her room, and as she got to her bed she started crying because she felt older and more fragile, as if someone had touched upon a particular chord in her, one whose existence she had denied until now.

Later in the night, when she heard his voice, she felt loneliness staring at her in a way that it never had before.

A Friend from London

She is sitting at the table of a restaurant on the Piazza Farnese in Rome. It is midday and the sun feels like hot wax on her porcelain skin. She stretches her legs out and looks at her perfectly manicured toenails framed by her Prada sandals. She is wearing a pale blue sleeveless dress, a straw hat and a pair of dark Gucci sunglasses that she picked up this morning on the via Condotti. She feels glamorous. The waiter walks towards her with a fixed smile on his face. He is wearing black pants, a white shirt and a shrivelled-up black bow tie. She orders a green salad and iced water. When he returns with her order, she notices he is sweating. 'Fa caldo oggi,' he says. She can only nod in agreement. The heat is making her feel slightly giddy, as if someone had knocked her over the head. She sips her iced water slowly and watches two children playing on the piazza. She plays with the ice cubes in her glass, twirling them around with her index finger. It is a habit that irritates Oliver.

She is happy with Oliver. They will be married in the autumn, and she wears his engagement ring proudly. A large diamond that sparkles in the midday sun. She never thought she'd get married so quickly. She had pictured herself going in and out of relationships, a revolving door of meetings and separations. She had never met a dependable man until Oliver. He is all she has ever wanted: strong, serious, pragmatic, a man for whom decisions carry few emotional consequences. When he asked her to marry him his tone was casual, as if he were asking her to go out to dinner. When she wiped away a few tears of joy, he hugged her tenderly. Then he went to the kitchen, pulled out a bottle of champagne from the refrigerator and they toasted each other a little clumsily, blushing almost. She remembers thinking that Oliver had never before looked so endearing to her as he did that day, standing sheepishly in his Savile Row suit, inadvertently spilling some champagne on his blue shirt.

Abigail feels secure with Oliver, content. She does not feel threatened by him, or out of control. She likes her emotions to be held in place like tightened bolts.

She moved in with Oliver shortly after they met, into his apartment overlooking Belgrave Square. He works for an investment bank. He often comes home late, finding her asleep in front of the television. She never protests about his working such long hours.

In meeting Oliver, a dark page in her life was turned. She can now focus on her new job, her impending married life, forget her past turmoils, the anxieties which used to wreak havoc in her life – misplacing objects, documents. She lost her wallet three times in one week. She didn't wake up for a breakfast meeting which could have launched her journalistic career. She missed several other appointments and assignments, causing her to be fired from one of her magazine jobs. She didn't show up for her first date with Oliver, confusing the day they were supposed to meet. Luckily, she bumped into him a few days later at a party where she was able to settle the matter diplomatically. He found her forgetfulness charming just when she had started to find it disturbing. His nonchalance allayed her anxieties. She never brought it up with him. And by keeping it inside, she convinced herself that she was cured. She respected Oliver, feared losing him. She found herself paying more attention to her surroundings, her gestures, her social interactions. She no longer left the house without checking her handbag and her notes for the day. She was, at last, becoming organized. Her love for Oliver was serene, comfortable, one of those things in life that made such perfect sense there was no need to question it.

The sound of a scooter interrupts her thoughts, suddenly a tall and robust man is standing near her, watching her twirl those same ice cubes absent-mindedly. She decides to ignore him and pulls out the notes she has jotted down for today's interview.

'Ciao bella, what is your name?' the man asks, pulling up a chair beside her.

'Excuse me?' She has found that making people repeat their sentences can sometimes be off-putting. But not to this man. He repeats his question, adding 'my lovely one', smiling at her broadly. He has striking green eyes, dark skin and a mischievous smile. He wears faded jeans, and a white T-shirt. He has unpolished good looks and peers at her imperiously through his dark lashes.

'My name is none of your business and someone is sitting here,' she replies, trying to sound as cold as possible.

'Someone is sitting here. Your husband?' He opens his eyes wide, chattering his teeth in mock fear. She finds him detestable.

She gathers together her belongings and gets up to

leave. She hails the waiter, motioning for the bill with her hand.

'I am Giacomo and you are English,' she hears the man say from somewhere behind her. 'I am sorry, I frighten you.' Vespas suddenly appear on the piazza, and a bevy of young men and women stand before her. They call Giacomo's name out. A brutish looking woman comes up to him and wraps her dark arms around his waist. 'Chi é?' She points towards Abigail, as if she were an inanimate object. 'Un amica di Londra,' she hears Giacomo tell her.

So there it is. She has become a friend from London. Curious the way strangers are able to find a common ground between themselves so rapidly, immediately setting the foundation for a friendship or a love affair. This ease of communication has lessened geographical and social boundaries, abrogating all need for protocol. This is something Oliver would agree with, and as she thinks about him, waking up next to him in their London apartment, she wishes he were with her. She misses him.

The same day Oliver proposed to her, Abigail received a phone call from Simon Barden. It was a phone call she had been anticipating, which confirmed her appointment as an assistant editor for the magazine she had been freelancing for. Abigail found out early on that fashion was her calling. She loved clothes. The texture of the materials. The different sensations silk or velvet created against her skin. The seams, darts and tucks she noticed when she bought a new piece of clothing and hung it in her packed wardrobe, some items still bearing sales tags. She felt that she understood clothes: the craftsmanship displayed on a perfectly cut bias; the social statements behind certain designs; how a pattern creates a mood. It was a dynamic business where an unknown designer from Norway could be propelled to fame from one day to the next. She wrote about it, and it wasn't long before she developed a good reputation among her peers.

Her parents weren't pleased with her decision. Her father had expected her to help out in his pharmaceutical company. She tried it out for a few months but was clearly unhappy. Her father urged her to stay longer, but she refused. She enrolled in art school. He saw it as a betrayal on her part. How could she study art? It was so futile, such a waste of time, he said to her. He threatened to stop talking to her.

But then he called back several days later, in a last attempt to patch things up between them. This time, Abigail was the one who told him that it was too late and now *she* was the one who felt that they had nothing further to discuss. Her father said 'very well then' and hung up. After that she didn't hear from him for several months. Now, thanks to Oliver, who formally asked her father for her hand, they are on speaking terms again. And the fact that her father approves of Oliver makes her happy.

After art school, Abigail attempted to create her own designs. They remained unnoticed. She decided that she preferred to write about fashion rather than create it. She found a job working for a magazine. There she remained until the magazine folded, landing a few freelance jobs after that. She had few friends in the industry. She kept to herself and went out in the evening with her old boarding-school friends. They thought of her as exotic and teased her about her work. She pretended that she didn't care. She longed to work for a renowned fashion magazine, and when the opportunity arose she bombarded the managing editor with phone calls, until he finally offered her the assignment she wanted. That was the part of her which always astonished Oliver – her perseverance, the fierce ambition she was capable of, a character trait which clashed oddly with her fragile physical appearance. When Simon Barden told her in an authoritative tone of voice, 'This assignment is your chance to prove yourself, we want you to fly to Rome and interview Andrea Mastero, the fashion designer,' she accepted enthusiastically. This was her big break. She had missed out on many professional chances in her life, and she was not about to let this one slip away.

The waiter brings her the bill and notices that she has left the salad untouched. She leaves too much money on the table and walks away rapidly. 'Aspetta!' Giacomo runs after her. 'I take you to see my beautiful city! My house has the most beautiful view! So much to see here! To talk about!'

'Talk? What in the world could we talk about?' she scoffs at him.

'But everything, cara mia! I want to know about you! Why are you in Italy for example?'

'I'm in Italy because I have an important job to do and I don't have time to talk to you right now. Goodbye.'

'Fine. Ciao. It is a pity. I have only good intentions,' he says, slapping his chest in a self-congratulatory way.

His remark causes her to smile. She detects something charming underneath his coarse face. She finds that she enjoys listening to his Italian accent in English. His pronunciation is seductive, and although he is obviously after her for one purpose only, she finds him, in an odd way, amusing. But these thoughts are quickly dispelled when she realizes that she has two hours left before her interview. She must get back to her hotel and study her notes, prepare the questions she will ask Andrea Mastero.

'Goodbye,' she tells Giacomo. 'And don't follow me.'

'Va be',' he answers, shrugging his shoulders in a childish way. 'Wait, wait!' He catches up with her. 'One more thing: if you want, I'll be in the piazza tonight,' he tells her, 'and then every day and every night after that.'

She conceals a smile. 'Goodbye,' she says again.

She walks away with self-imposed confidence, clutching her handbag. She doesn't turn around. She wonders if Giacomo is following her. It is all a little worrisome and, at the same time, a little exciting. She wonders if anything like this has ever happened to any of her friends. They all share similar backgrounds. They grew up in affluent families, studied hard and are now mostly married or engaged, some with children. She's the product of a predictable environment. She has never felt rebellious. The idea of breaking loose never tempted her. She doesn't like to lose control. Oliver feels the same way. Actually, she and Oliver have many ideas in common, that's what attracted her to him in the first place – and his looks, which she finds dashing, although her best friend Polly has confessed to finding him banal-looking. But Polly never had good taste in men.

She hails a taxi. She will call Oliver when she gets to the hotel. She wants to speak to him, hear his reassuring voice. Not like that vulgar Giacomo. She turns around before getting into the taxi. He has obviously given up on following her. Good riddance.

She calls Oliver. She tells him about her morning, about the sunglasses she purchased. She doesn't tell him about Giacomo.

Oliver sounds busy on the phone and asks her to call him later. She hangs up, disappointed. She had expected him to sound more enthusiastic.

She sits on her bed, studying the questions she will ask Andrea Mastero. She changes into a red Mastero suit, with matching high-heeled shoes. She checks the hotel room several times before finally closing the door. She has everything: the tape-recorder, the notes, the address and phone number.

Andrea Mastero's house is far from the hotel, tucked away in a peaceful tree-lined street. His house is decorated lavishly. The ceilings and walls are all gilded, and in the middle of the living room stands a marble fountain. The designer himself sits like an emperor in a large armchair, upholstered with his own material. Mastero is overweight and looks tired. As his hands rest on the armchair, Abigail notices his fingernails. They are long and buffed, with only a faint trace of nail polish. She wonders which brand he uses, but keeps the thought to herself.

At one point during the interview, while Andrea is describing the different textiles he has found in Morocco and other exotic countries (he is flying to Morocco tomorrow morning, he wants to buy himself a house in Marrakesh), Abigail finds herself thinking about Giacomo. This disturbs her and she forces herself to focus on Mastero's words.

He responds to all her questions diligently, occasionally carrying on for too long. As she leaves his house, Abigail realizes that this interview has gone very well, beyond her wildest expectations. She will do a good job. Barden and his colleagues will not regret their decision to hire her.

She jumps into the cab Mastero has called for her. She plays back some of the interview. The questions are concise and to the point. When she arrives at the hotel, she immediately calls the magazine. Simon Barden tells her to start transcribing it all. She hangs up feeling elated. She tries Oliver again but this time he is away from his desk.

She reaches out for her bag. As she picks it up she notices that it feels lighter. She finds her wallet and her notes. She reaches her hand further in, then in a desperate gesture pours all the contents on to the bed. Her compact, her lipstick, her plane tickets and passport come tumbling down, but not the tape-recorder. She has lost it. She must have left it in the taxi.

She immediately calls Andrea Mastero and asks for the phone number of the taxi company. 'I misplaced something,' she tells him. He gives her the number and she dials anxiously. A man answers the phone, and she finds herself stammering. Her Italian is very rudimentary, and the same could be said about the man's English. She runs downstairs and tells the hotel manager about her plight. He kindly calls back the cab company and explains what has happened. The dispatcher tells him that they haven't found anything, but if they do they will call him. Assolutamente.

Abigail runs up to her room and starts to cry. She calls Oliver. He is still out. She flings herself on the bed. She has done it again. She cannot call Simon and tell him. She cannot call anybody. She must wait in her hotel room and assail the cab company with calls until they find the tape-recorder. They must find it. Unless, of course, the cab driver or one of his passengers purloined it, in which case her efforts will have been in vain. She cannot call Andrea Mastero again. Besides, he is off to Morocco tomorrow, there is no time left for another interview.

She waits, seated on the bed. At around eight o'clock, she goes to the front desk and asks the hotel manager to ring up the taxi company again. He does so, although reluctantly. He dials slowly and sighs while they put him on hold. She can hear the music streaming through the receiver. She attempts a half-hearted smile for the manager, who returns a cold stare. 'I am a busy man at this moment,' he tells her. She hears the gruff voice of the cab company manager – no they haven't found any tape-recorder and, yes, of course they will call if they do.

She goes up to her room and changes into a pair of black Capri pants, black moccasins and a striped black and white shirt she bought in a second-hand shop in Notting Hill, where she used to live. She grabs her Indian handbag, slams the door of her hotel room and hails a taxi. She asks the taxi-driver to drop her off at the Piazza Farnese. She goes back to the restaurant. There is a large group of people gathered around the French Institute. Many of them are talking on cellular telephones, waving their arms emphatically. Somebody is playing loud music, although Abigail cannot place where it is coming from. The restaurant is much more crowded than it was at midday and the waiters are different. She orders a glass of wine and drinks it rapidly. A warm sensation rises in her legs. She sits there for a long time and pulls the morning's *Herald Tribune* out of her handbag. She glances at it distractedly. She feels something on her arm; a ladybird is crawling up her elbow. Its red and black dots remind her of a coat she bought last winter. She lets the ladybird fall on to the table. Then suddenly, in a rash gesture, she crushes it under her thumb. It makes a crackling sound like a nut being opened, she sees its wings flatten out like an aeroplane. She crushes it again with all her might until the body distintegrates, a drop of blood smears on to the table, and this time she shivers with horror at what she has just done. She brushes the dead insect off the table with her newspaper. Her neck feels ice cold and her hand is trembling uncontrollably. She glances around her. No one seems to have noticed anything. She is suddenly very thirsty and orders another glass of wine. One of the waiters asks her if she'd like anything to eat. She shakes her head and attempts to say 'no grazie', but the words get caught in her throat.

She tries to read the newspaper again. At one point, she looks up and sees Giacomo. He is holding a young woman's hand, a beautiful woman in her early twenties. The woman places her body against Giacomo's and seems to whisper something in his ear. He lifts her up and they both start laughing, a fresh and melodic laughter that stabs Abigail's heart in an unexpected way. The girl walks away and Giacomo remains still, waving at her and shouting something Abigail cannot hear. The realization of what she is doing – anticipating the attentions of a stranger in a foreign land – hits her so hard that she attempts to hide behind some customers when she sees Giacomo walking towards her. But it is too late. He has seen her. She pays her bill quickly and gets up, but this time he orders her to sit back down. 'Stay. Have a drink with me. I am happy to see you. I was waiting for you. I knew you would come back here. You have beautiful lips,' he adds, bringing his face closer to hers. She lowers her eyes. Oliver never speaks to her like that.

She asks him about the girl she saw him with. He tells her that she is his fiancée, and they will be married in April. This reassures her. At least the man has some semblance of normality about him. She finds herself telling him about what happened to her, about Oliver, about how he will react to the latest events. 'I've jeopardized my future,' she tells him. 'What does that mean?' he asks her. She explains. He volunteers something about her sounding confused. 'Somewhere in your pretty English head you create chaos. But I think that is good. A healthy sign. We Italians like chaos. And we like the English too . . .' A soft smile forms on his lips, and she wonders again what she's doing there with him. If Oliver saw her now, he'd be shocked. Giacomo asks her if she'd like to go for a drive. She hesitates. 'You have nothing to lose any more, no?' he asks her as she climbs on to the back of his motorcycle. She can only nod her head because he has taken the words right out of her mouth.

He caresses her and rolls his tongue in her mouth and undresses her quickly, passing his hands along the contours of her body. She meekly attempts to push him away.

He licks the nipples of her breasts and shoves his hand deep between her legs. Her eyes remain open because it keeps pleasure at bay.

Her body has become malleable between his hands and she lets him explore it in ways no one has ever done before.

She doesn't realize her eyes have been closed until he throws her on his bed and mounts her, holding her wrists down as she screams something about him killing her.

Later in the night, he takes her in his arms, drops her gently on the soft carpet and enters her from behind while holding her tightly against him until she gasps for air. She screams again and he covers her mouth with his rugged hands. She bites him hard and he pushes her away brusquely. 'Strónza,' he hisses. 'Crazy English girl.' She tells him she wants to go back to her hotel. She puts her clothes back on, feeling his sweat against her, she is repulsed now, she feels like vomiting all over him.

She leaves his apartment, slamming the door loudly behind her. She walks for a long time in the dark streets before finding a taxi. When she arrives at the hotel, there is a note on her door saying that the cab company manager has called. They have not recovered the tape-recorder. There are also three notes saying that Oliver has called, and to please call him back the minute she gets home.

She takes a long shower and washes her hair. She wants to feel clean before talking to Oliver. She lies on her bed and dials the number slowly. So slowly that the call doesn't go through. She decides to wait a little and try again in the morning. She walks to her window and looks outside. The sun is rising slowly. Outside, the air is fresh and still. She closes the window and walks back to her bed. She keeps the phone on her chest, peering at the numbers on the dial until they become a blur. She falls asleep to the sound of bells ringing in a nearby church.

Before Berlin

Helen was surprised but happy when she found out she was pregnant, although her joy was tainted with an apprehension of it happening perhaps too soon after the birth of their fifteen-month-old son – an apprehension which she shoved away somewhere in the back of her mind, like a book she might pick up later on when there was more time to focus on it.

When she looked at her face in the mirror she saw it glow, the way it had when she was expecting Jonas, and when she felt a pang of nausea, she welcomed it with a smile.

She wondered how Peter would react once she broke the news to him. They hadn't really discussed another child, except to say that they eventually wanted a sibling for Jonas, but these were only plans they hadn't had any intention of realizing so soon.

Helen approached Peter as he was making himself a cup of tea in the kitchen.

I'm pregnant, she told him, trying to sound as nonchalant as possible.

What do you mean, you're pregnant?

Just that. I'm pregnant.

I see. Well, shit. Peter looked at her inquisitively. This is all a bit sudden isn't it?

It is, yes. Sudden and unexpected. She looked at him,

watching him pour the boiling water into his cup, letting a tea bag float on the surface.

How do you feel about it? he asked, after removing the tea bag and throwing it into the rubbish bin.

I think I'm happy about it, she answered after a long pause.

You think or you know?

I know, she said resolutely.

I see.

He was silent again. When he turned his face towards her, it was to reveal a grave expression, one that he only bore at critical times.

I don't know about this, Helen. You're really catching me off guard here. You see, I'm not sure I'm happy about you being pregnant, and I'm not sure we can handle another child just yet.

I can handle it, she answered assuredly.

Yes, but I don't think I can. And I'm not sure you can either, he added, his brown eyes fixing hers, his fingers clutching the handle of his tea mug.

Oh, is that so? Helen asked defensively. At that point she realized that the whole issue was going to put her on the defensive, rendering all rational discussion useless.

Yes, it is so, and I certainly don't want to start arguing about this, he said. And by the way, how come you got pregnant? I thought we had been careful and all of that . . .

I suppose nature doesn't always go by the *all of that* rule, does it?

Nature is not the only one responsible here, is it?

I have no idea, she answered haughtily.

Well, I guess it's bad timing, he answered with one of those forced smiles of his which she found irritating.

Where's Jonas?

Sleeping, she answered

I'm out of cigarettes. I'll be right back.

She heard Peter run down the stairs and on to the street. She looked out of the window and saw him go into the Indian shop across the street, where Mrs Kumar, wearing one of her colourful saris, would hand him his cigarettes without a word. That was the nature of their relations, ever since she had caught Peter buying those same cigarettes twice in one week from the rival shop at the end of the road. Mrs Kumar had taken personal offence at his gesture, she who was so careful to stock all the items he required, from his favourite crackers, to the special orange juice for Mrs and the special sweeties for the little one, she who priced her wares so reasonably, while Mr Shankar swindled his clients with his high prices and his big ugly smile which took up all of his face.

When Peter confessed that actually Mr Shankar's cigarettes were twenty pence cheaper than hers, Mrs Kumar's face turned bright red and she asked Peter to leave the shop immediately. This was obviously her way of dealing with affront, and Peter let her release her steam in a torrent of words, which he heard all the way down the street as she stormed into Mr Shankar's shop, her strident voice resonating above the heavy traffic.

Ever since then Peter had attempted to make amends with Mrs Kumar, but she refused to budge. Her husband, an older man with a sweaty brow, assured Peter that she would soon resume cordial relations with him. She's a woman, you know, he said to Peter one morning, you have to give women time. Not like us men. Then he laughed loudly and Peter laughed with him.

The incident caused Helen to frequent the shop less often than she had, and both she and Peter hoped Mrs Kumar would get over the humiliation she claimed her shameless patron had made her suffer.

As she was looking out of the window, Helen suddenly heard a child crying loudly, insistently, for his mother. It was only after a few long minutes that she realized the child was Jonas, and he was screaming at the top of his lungs in his attic bedroom, begging for her, begging for someone to come and comfort him.

She rushed upstairs. When she got to his bedroom, Jonas had fallen asleep, and his wet pillow was testimony to his desperate cries which had gone unanswered.

She found herself trembling as she walked out of his bedroom. Once again, she had arrived too late. Whereas Peter was able to foresee problems ahead of time, Helen couldn't. And her lack of forethought made both her and Peter suffer.

This eventually put a strain on their marriage, and they sought out a marriage counsellor shortly after Jonas's birth.

You have to pay more attention, the counsellor told Helen. And you have to be more patient, she told Peter.

The counsellor's bill was high and her words got lost in the days and months that followed their short therapy sessions.

Only later did Helen realize that although the marriage counsellor had asked her a few questions about her upbringing, Helen had failed to tell her the extent of the pain she had suffered during her parents' divorce, when her father had walked out on her mother, her older brother Tim and thirteen-year-old Helen. She could distinctly remember when at around eight o'clock one morning she heard her parents screaming at each other, not an unusual occurrence since high-pitched voices and verbal abuse had become their main means of communication by then.

The previous evening, her father had told Helen that he was off to Berlin the next day, where he had an important business meeting. Tim had warned Helen that whenever he used the words *business meeting* she should be aware that it was a code name for a woman, a revelation Helen found too extraordinary to dwell upon. Her mother and father might disagree, but they were a family unit and nothing, not even verbal abuse, was going to change that notion.

But this time, when her father put his warm hand around her neck and uttered those fateful words, Helen felt that she should say something. She cleared her throat and let out the words, what's her name? before she could control the speed at which they were released.

Her father answered that he didn't know who she was referring to. Who are you talking about? he asked her. She could see that he had a tense expression on his face which he was trying to mould into a smile.

Never mind, she said, although she wanted to say so much more to him.

She felt like crying and she told her father that she hoped he would come home soon. Of course I will! he exclaimed, what is going on with you?

He left their Primrose Hill house and never came back.

Her mother told both her children that she didn't want their father's name uttered in the household. The less we talk about him, the better off we will be and the easier it will be to forget him.

Helen found it hard to tell her mother that she didn't want to forget him, so Tim told her instead.

You can see him on your own, she said, shrugging her shoulders. That louse. That pig. That pervert.

They obeyed their mother and mentioned him only to each other. They mourned his loss together. Then one day, shortly after his departure, he wrote them separate letters explaining that he had met another woman, was now living in Berlin and was looking forward to seeing them the following weekend. He had enclosed two tickets in the envelopes. When Tim and Helen boarded the plane and landed at Berlin airport, the man they saw walking towards them was not the same man they had loved and grown up with in Primrose Hill.

But this was a realization that neither of them was able to verbalize because there was doubt in both of their minds as to how objective they were being, considering the circumstances in which they were seeing him again. Before Berlin, he had been their loving father who, even during those difficult times when he and Mother didn't get along, always took time to be with the children and to teach them what he called facts of life, facts of nature and facts of the world.

Now, the man standing before them seemed dishevelled and ill at ease, as if he didn't know how to behave with his own children any more, as if he were embarrassed to see them. And there was nothing in the world which hurt Helen more than that painful sight.

When he bent over to kiss Tim, the latter pushed him away. Are you going to be teaching us about the facts of separation now? he asked brusquely.

Yes, actually, I was planning on it, their father answered with remarkable calm.

Later on he explained his departure and Helen pretended to listen, although under her long hair she was plugging her ears and concentrating her thoughts on London and her girlfriend Tessa who had just got her first period and whose father was bringing her to a Rolling Stones concert where they would be sitting in a private box because their manager was a friend of his.

Helen found that the habits she acquired during her parents separation were too difficult to shed, however hard she tried. They had become part of her persona, and somewhere they even felt comforting, like an old friend she could always rely upon. Whenever she was hurt or angry she could feel her emotions stack up inside her like an overflowing cupboard, and she could think of no other option but to keep them to herself. Unleashing them would reveal wounds she didn't feel able to confront.

But Peter felt otherwise. Ever since she had met him, four years back, he had been slowly but surely prying open that overflowing cupboard of hers. Although she desperately tried to cling to her pain as though it were hers alone and no one else's, she could feel it unleashing on its own, beyond her control and beyond her will, and the feeling was not all that unpleasant. Actually, and this was to her surprise, it was something of a relief.

But now, she felt quite different: it was up to her to make the decision, to do the right thing. She knew Peter would support her, yet she also knew that however much she wanted this child, it was not the right time. Helen had to prove Peter wrong, show him she was a responsible adult, not the child he often accused her of being. She was capable of limiting damage, or preventing it, before it was too late. She was happy in her marriage, she loved Peter and the security he gave her, the space he provided for her.

She dialled the doctor's office slowly. His secretary answered the phone.

This is Helen Marden, I'd like to book an appointment with Dr Rodgers, she said, trying to keep her voice from trembling.

Is this for a check up? the secretary asked in a tired voice.

A pregnancy, Helen answered cautiously.

Congratulations, Helen! the secretary exclaimed, her voice more cheerful.

Helen hung up quickly. She heard Peter's footsteps coming up the stairs. When he appeared at the door, he had a gleeful smile on his face.

What is it? she asked him with some trepidation.

Mrs Kumar told me to have a good day, and of course a very good day to the Mrs she said. She also asked me to give this to Jonas.

Peter handed her a chocolate bar which she gazed at pensively. Soon, Jonas would wake up, his little face warm from sleep, his skin soft like velvet, his eyes shining like diamonds. He would coo like a bird and she would hold him tenderly against her chest. Soon.

A Matter of Time

Penelope and Hugo's guests are starting to leave the party. It is late. Sometime after midnight and before morning. The room is very dark. There is a strong feeling of over-indulgence hanging in the air. The stale cigarette smells. The unfinished joint in a filled ashtray. Traces of cocaine on a glass surface. The many empty liquor bottles. The way the guests move about the room like puppets on strings, dragging their words with tired lips.

In Penelope and Hugo's room everything is clean. Here the smells are expensive. A sweetly scented candle. Opulent leather armchairs. Crisp white linen sheets that smell of country air. Rows and rows of impeccably folded clothes that fill the lavender-scented made-to-measure closets in their dressing room.

Miranda uses Penelope's bathroom. Her head feels heavy, her thoughts are light, her breath is sour. She flushes the toilet and notices that her stockings have a run. She adjusts them clumsily.

She thinks of Hugo. She finds him very attractive. She wants him. She feels the urge to brush her teeth. She uses Penelope's toothbrush, she will never know. Then she puts it down quickly, feeling that she has just done something terribly wrong.

She can hear her husband's voice behind the bedroom door. He is talking to Phaedra, a Greek actress with long frizzy hair and a bad nose job. 'Give me a call in the morning, I'll see what I can do,' she hears Ben tell her. How many times has she heard that sentence? She can picture Ben handing over his business card, Phaedra receiving it gracefully, reading his phone number with exaggerated concentration. 'That's so sweet of you,' she hears her tell him. 'Not at all,' Ben answers. Then Miranda hears him calling out her name. 'Miranda? Where are you?'

Miranda opens the bedroom door where her husband is standing. 'Let's go home, I've had it with this party,' he tells her.

'What's with the Greek vamp?' Miranda asks him. 'You want to further her film career?'

Ben smiles. 'Hugo wants me to see what I can do. He says she's good. Come to think of it, I'm surprised Hugo even knows people like Phaedra. Probably does some Athenian humpy-pumpy with her. Can't think of any other reason why she would be here.'

'She's David Green's girlfriend.' Miranda sighs in an irritated way. 'And what in the world does humpy-pumpy mean? It sounds ridiculous.'

Ben laughs loudly and puts his arm around her neck. 'I find it hilarious. Miranda, darling, you don't know how much I enjoy mumping, sorry, humping-pumping you.'

'Shut up, you're being stupid. And you're embarrassing me.' She pushes him away. His breath smells of alcohol and he is speaking too loudly. She clutches the banister as Ben follows her down the stairs. The sitting room seems more crowded. Miranda feels slightly dizzy. She has had too much to drink. She hopes that Hugo hasn't heard what Ben has just said to her.

David Green walks over to them. 'I've got to get out of here. It's two in the morning, I'm drunk out of my wits and I've got an eight o'clock conference call. Big merger happening tomorrow morning, Ben. And look at me now. A basket case.'

'That's great. Nice girlfriend you have there,' Ben says, patting David on the back. 'See you soon, buddy.' He turns towards Miranda. 'Let's go,' he says, 'it's late.'

They kiss their hosts goodbye. They walk to their car in silence. Ben drives away rapidly.

'Quite a party that was,' Miranda hears him say.

'Yes,' she answers, her voice feeling raspy and sore, 'that was a great party and I'm wasted.'

'I'm glad you had a good time,' Ben says, in an inscrutable tone of voice.

'Why do you say that? Didn't you have a good time?'

'Oh, I had a great time,' he answers firmly.

'That's good. Penelope and Hugo are really nice.'

'Hugo thinks the same of you. It's quite apparent. Quite touching, I might add.'

'Oh, please.' Miranda laughs nervously. 'Actually,' she adds, her voice sounding suddenly nonchalant and chirpy, 'it's a pity I find him so annoying.'

'I find him perfectly charming,' Ben answers, keeping his eyes on the road, 'and I believe that you do too. Why wouldn't you? All the women are in love with Hugo. At least, that's what I'm told.'

'Oh, come on, Ben.' She puts her arm around his shoulder and kisses his cheek. 'You're not going to tell me that you're jealous, are you?' she asks him in a teasing voice.

'Absolutely, yes,' Ben answers as he parks the car in their tree-lined street. 'I love the fact that my wife, who's given me children and is nearing her forty-second birthday, is as desirable to men as when I rescued her from the depths of misery she was living in.'

'Don't exaggerate, Ben. I never lived in misery.'

'No, of course not, my darling.' His tone is cold, and his comments hurt her, as they often do, but she chooses to remain diplomatically quiet. He is only provoking her and she is too tired to argue with him.

They climb the staircase to their bedroom. They wash their faces in separate sinks. They lie side by side in bed, a thick duvet covering their cold bodies. They do not embrace as they usually do. As Miranda falls asleep, Hugo invades her last waking moments; he is standing by her, soon he will kiss her, it is only a matter of time. Something disrupts the image. Not her conscience, but a child's cry – Mummy, Mummy, the wolf is in my bedroom with his green eyes. Her son Patrick is standing there in his little flannel pyjamas. She hugs and kisses him and brings him back up to his warm bed. They fall asleep together, his little breath close to her skin, his hand entwined in hers.

Hugo is standing in the kitchen. The guests have just finished eating their dinner. There are vast quantities of food left. Penelope always orders too much food. Hugo takes a mouthful of a red-looking gratin dish. He cannot, for the life of him, remember what it is. This time Penelope used a renowned chef, but Hugo is too drunk to tell the difference. It tastes like sawdust to him. Actually, Hugo doesn't even remember why they are having such an elaborate party. With such an eclectic mix of people. Very unlike Penelope. Very daring of her. With all that cocaine circulating, all that booze. Perhaps Penelope is going through one of those mid-life crises. She needs to reinvent herself, project a less rigid image. Penelope the new woman.

Ah! Now he remembers why they had the party. Andrew Spencer's birthday party. Penelope loves Andrew, her oldest friend. She should have married him instead. She could have had a properly boring life with him. Then again, hold on. She has a properly boring life with Hugo. Why would she want to replicate boredom? Indeed. Why? Ha, ha, ha.

Hugo looks over at Penelope. Her face is squashed like a furry animal. 'Squish, squish, little animal, my own wife. Hee, hee, hee, boom-boom, bim, bim, boom.'

'Talking to yourself, Hugo?' It is Sylvia, Andrew's wife. She has bright blue eyeshadow on her lids and unevenly shaped rosy lips. 'Great party. Delightful. I love your producer friend. Such an interesting man. I don't know about his wife but I find him absolutely charming. Here, have a smoke.' She hands over a joint, he takes a short puff and hands it back to her. 'Thank you, thank you, boom-boom-boom.' Sylvia looks at him strangely and walks away.

He is going mad. His life is closing in on him and he needs Miranda to escape. He pours himself another drink. He glances over at Miranda who is distractedly flipping through a book. She is beautiful and graceful, and when she looks at him it makes his heart sink. Whenever they talk to each other they bump into each other's words and laugh together awkwardly. He feels as if he's known her for ever and has told her as much. She smiles and blushes lightly, as she does whenever he talks to her. He notices that she cannot keep her gaze focused on his, and this gives him hope. Whereas he previously thought that she disdained him, he has now realized that she desires him just as much as he does her. Tonight, as someone was passing a joint around, she reclined on the white sofa with a sigh and stretched out her long legs. She laughed, for no reason in particular and he understood that she was stoned. He sat down next to her and took her hand in his. 'This woman drives me wild,' he told his guests. Somehow, he thought that advertising his attraction to her in public would obviate what he felt for her in private. It was no longer a secret, but something they could all joke about, without it having any concrete consequences. Except that when they had all finished joking about how Ben was a lucky bastard, Hugo realized that Miranda's fingers had now interlaced themselves between his. Her face was calm and her voice steady. Her body was pressed next to his, her long hair partially covering her profile. He wanted her to turn around and look at him. Confirm that this was not an empathic gesture, but a sexual one which he could carry further. He attempted to speak to her but she was in deep conversation with Emma, talking about her daughter's primary school.

'They put so much pressure on these poor children,' he heard Miranda say. 'Caroline always looks so exhausted when she comes home from school.'

Hugo gently removed his hand from hers. 'I've got to

check on the wine,' he said to her. He got up and walked away. She didn't even seem to acknowledge his departure, continuing her conversation in the same steady tone.

Penelope walked over to both women and tucked her skirt in carefully as she sat down next to Miranda. Although she was high as a kite, Penelope still cared about manners.

Hugo heard them all laugh at the same time and a sudden fear overtook him. He was in love with Miranda and she was going to ruin his life with Penelope. He could foresee their future together, an ephemeral passion that would turn into mutual resentment. The same could be said about Penelope, although the resentment had given way to a placid indifference. And there was something comfortable about that indifference, because neither of them expected anything from each other. They had everything they needed. He was a successful property developer. They had a house in Kensington. Two grown boys in boarding school. They spent weekends at their country cottage. Their bickering was appropriately domestic, and their social life revolved around the same faces and places. 'We're self-indulgent materialists,' Penelope had recently said, to Hugo's horror, because up until then, he hadn't thought of his life as self-indulgent but as sound. Just like his father and mother. He had followed in their footsteps because early on he had been taught that if you have the means, you should thank the Lord for having them. Be righteous and rigorous, and never swerve from your chosen path.

But for some time now, Hugo's path had been swerving. He couldn't pinpoint why it was. Perhaps it was his love for Penelope that was slowly dwindling away. It had veered from comfortable indifference to unsettling restlessness. He felt like a child who cannot stop himself from climbing over a forbidden fence. What he was about to discover, he wasn't sure. All he knew was that he could no longer curb his impulse.

He didn't mention any of this to Penelope, and she didn't seem to notice any changes in him. 'I know you so well, I don't notice you any more,' she often told him.

The same could not be said of Hugo. He noticed Penelope. He knew her well. He had quietly observed her new fondness for cocaine. She was bored, she told Hugo, and a little sniff here and there was not going to kill her. Her friends were doing the same. At least now she had a reason for sleeping late in the morning, whereas before she didn't. Penelope liked to have a reason for everything. Without it, she felt out of kilter, as if her life had no purpose. Hugo couldn't argue with that. He felt the same way. So for the sake of his marriage, he didn't question Penelope's choices in life and he never cheated on her. Not because he didn't want to, but because the occasion, though it had presented itself numerous times, never seemed worth it. The women he knew were all predictable. If he was going to cheat on his wife, it had to be with someone special.

And now he had found her. He had told Ben as much. Crazy man he was, to tell Miranda's own husband what he thought of his lovely wife. He liked Ben, although he found him too aloof. Ben was richer than all of them combined and he was the stingiest one of all. Hugo had met both of them at a cocktail party. Miranda and Penelope had immediately become friends, though Hugo wondered what they found in common. They were very different women, and Penelope seemed to take pride in that. 'I love our new trendy friends, a breath of fresh air from the usual pale faces we always hang around with, although, mind you, I love our pale-faced friends.' Then she had laughed uneasily and he had laughed uneasily back. Hugo could tell that Ben didn't like Penelope, but he didn't care. He didn't mind seeing Ben on his own. Except that Ben cancelled two of their lunch meetings. So they stuck to their nocturnal mingling, only once venturing out to a Thai restaurant where both couples split the bill. Ben's films made millions and he always called them flops. 'What don't you call a flop?' Hugo had once asked him, and Ben had laughed off his question with a forgettable non sequitur.

Ben was possessive of Miranda, who had once been a model. Now she was the mother of two beautiful children and had given up modelling. She had taken up acting, at the age of forty-two. She loved it, she said, and Hugo believed her.

Yes, he believed in her even though he hardly knew her. Her talent, her beauty, her sadness, her fragility. He watched Miranda pull herself off the white sofa and walk self-consciously towards the bar. She poured herself a glass of water and licked the tip of her index finger for no obvious reason. She drank rapidly and put the glass back down. Her large eyes gazed at Hugo as he walked over to her. 'Have lunch with me tomorrow,' he found himself imploring her. 'Please. I've got to see you alone. One o'clock at my office.'

'All right,' she answered softly, before walking away.

She arrived at Hugo's office, her cheeks red, her hair loose. She wore a black skirt and a white blouse. A heavy gold choker wrapped around her slender neck. She fumbled over her words when she saw him and lit a cigarette before sitting down. They spoke of the weather and of the trip Hugo and Penelope were planning to China.

Miranda's mobile phone rang. She spoke quickly, in monosyllables. Hugo felt like asking her who it was. Then his phone rang and he excused himself before taking a business call. 'I've got to take this one, it will only be a minute,' he told her. On the phone, his voice sounded confident, cold and pragmatic. Miranda felt gypped. He was like all the other men she had ever known. None of them were consistent in their behaviour. They all adjusted their manner according to the situation they found themselves in. So did Ben, and so did Hugo. The thought that she did the same didn't occur to her.

When he hung up, Hugo asked her where she wanted to have lunch. Miranda told him he could choose. He took her to Nobu. She hated Japanese food, but that was just as well because she was too nervous to eat anything. She ordered a salad. He started talking about his son's boarding school. She didn't listen to anything he said. She was trying to make herself feel disillusioned.

'I'm asking you a question,' she heard him say. She raised her eyes towards him.

'I'm sorry, I didn't hear you.'

'That's all right. Unimportant question, anyway. So' – he moved closer towards her and gave her a beautiful smile – 'how are you? How's your acting going?'

'Fine, I guess.' She fidgeted and took a little sip of

water. She felt tense. This wasn't right. 'This isn't right,' she heard herself saying, although she wondered how she mustered the courage to reveal the truth when all she wanted was to conceal her weakness.

'It's not about being right,' Hugo answered, 'it's about something we both want.' She found his declaration shocking. Not because of its meaning, but because he was able to say it so casually, with such ease. He had said too much, uttered too many words. Perhaps she had triggered it, but he had gone too far. She had liked the tension between them: the excitement mounting, the mystery of whether or not he felt the same about her. Now, he had broken the spell. Maybe it was just as well. She had a family, a husband who loved her. There was no reason for this to happen. She wasn't dissatisfied with her marriage. Misunderstood at times. But everybody was. She just had to work on getting things straight with Ben. It was hard to talk to him, because he always brushed off her recriminations. He never seemed to take her seriously. 'You have a charmed life,' he would say in an accusing tone, 'there's no reason for you to be unhappy.'

She seldom disagreed with him. She had a fear of disagreements, going back to when she was a little girl. So she often gave in to his demands because it was easier that way. But that would have to change. Yes, she would make it change. There was no reason why she couldn't. She was stronger than she appeared to be. Hugo seemed to sense that. But she would have to forget about Hugo. Her feelings for him would die down eventually.

She felt better now. She started talking about her children, about her acting. Hugo listened attentively. This wasn't easy. For either of them. The prospect of hurting their spouses was daunting. Unnecessary perhaps. He was going to have to suppress his desire, focus on something other than a woman. A sport perhaps. Yes, good idea. He would call Andrew in the morning and have a game of tennis with him. Brilliant idea. He needed to get some new tennis shoes. He had left his previous ones in Greece, where they had spent last summer with the boys. Wonderful holiday. Except for Penelope's terrible sunburn.

Miranda's phone rang again. Then, it stopped. She shrugged her shoulders and smiled at him. Finally, a smile. Never mind if she made him melt, if he wanted to grab her gold choker and press her against him. It was best to leave it be. Hugo ordered the bill. 'Let's go,' he said.

She followed him out of the restaurant. It had started to rain.

They joked on the street. About the party, about Andrew and Sylvia. Nothing better than gossip in order to diffuse tension. Hugo found himself walking towards the car. 'I'll drive you home,' he said. She appeared surprised. 'You don't need to do that.'

'I'd love to do it.'

They drove away in the rain. He put some music on. She was seated near him, he could smell her perfume. She was looking straight in front of her. She could feel his presence near her. It made her happy. At one point he stopped and looked at her. She looked back. He parked the car in a busy street. She didn't ask him why. He brought his lips against hers. She tasted like the pulp of a fruit. He couldn't have enough of her. She surrendered to him.

Later, his head lost somewhere in the thick of her hair, he whispered something about it being the end of an era. In his arms she remained, as the thick raindrops beat against the window pane.